Eat, Drink, and Be Buried

Also by Peter King

The Gourmet Detective
Spiced to Death
Dying on the Vine
Death al Dente
A Healthy Place to Die

Peter King

Eat, Drink, and Be Buried

A Gourmet Detective Mystery

ST. MARTIN'S MINOTAUR ♉ NEW YORK

www.minotaurbooks.com

ISBN 0-312-24270-0

First Edition: May 2001

10 9 8 7 6 5 4 3 2 1

Eat, Drink, and Be Buried

CHAPTER ONE

The two eyed one another, warily, like tigers before a fight. Silence hung heavily all around them, disturbed only by a faint metallic clink. The hushed ambiance bristled with bloodthirsty anticipation, prickling like sweat on a muggy day.

There was no movement except for the flags, dazzling in scarlet, black, and gold. They whipped languidly against their posts.

The first sound came like trumpets, shrill and clear, as sharply authoritative as barked parade ground orders. The two stirred, getting positioned, oriented, lining up like sharpshooters on a target.

The quiet that followed was like a great blanket of snow, then the trumpet notes slashed out again but sounding different this time. The two erupted into motion.

Slowly at first, then gaining momentum, they raced toward each other, faster and faster, hurtling forward like projectiles.

Sound swelled up from every corner now. Voices urged on the two, strident and screeching, many infused with a lust for blood. Every eye was intent on the combatants, gleaming with expectancy. Fists shook in encouragement, arms waved wildly.

The ground began to shake and the roar of the crowd swelled. The clanking and snorting could hardly be heard over the noise of the spectators. The combatants rushed toward each other at dazzling speed, metal juggernauts on a collision course that could end only in death and disaster.

———

Harlington Castle had begun to stage its "Medieval Days" about ten years earlier. First it had been banquets, then the jousts and the tournaments were added and were an immediate success. The accouterments of the Middle Ages followed—the fairs, the animals, the village with its glassblowers and blacksmiths, its potters and weavers, the wandering minstrels, the jugglers and stilt walkers, the midgets and the dwarfs.

The castle itself was the last feature to be brought from the sixteenth century to the twenty-first century. The music room rang once more with the notes of the clavichord and the cembalo, the harp and the cremona. The kitchens were equipped with every modern device, but the appearance of older times was maintained. As for the meals the kitchens produced . . . that was where I came in.

I am a food-finder. I locate hard-to-find food ingredients, I track down rare herbs and spices, and seek out substitutes for foods that have become expensive or unobtainable. A newspaper columnist wrote an article on me and dubbed me "The Gourmet Detective." The only detecting I did was in the kitchen, the herb garden, and the delicatessen—at least, that was how it was supposed to be. The fabric of life is inextricably interwoven with food and cooking, however, and now and then I would find myself embroiled in cases that led to theft, trickery, and even murder.

Another of my activities which I particularly enjoy is that I am often called upon to advise on meals to suit special occasions. In this case, the occasion was the Middle Ages. Initially, Harlington Castle had served fairly simple meals that reflected the comparatively simple times. Roast baron of beef, roast chicken, potatoes, and everyday vegetables like peas and carrots had comprised the bill of fare.

A change had to be made when portions of the castle were restored to provide accommodation. In many European countries, old manorhouses, monasteries, and abbeys had been converted into pleasant hotels that still had the feeling of tradition and a few crumbling walls for confirming effect. Some of these had become havens of good food and sophisticated cooking.

Harlington Castle now provided charming and spacious rooms furnished with antiques, tapestries, and carpets, but still incorporating every modern convenience. Such accommodation, they decided, required food of a comparative quality, and they determined to offer the same quality in the banquet room as they did in the castle dining room.

So the chicken and the beef had to go, in their more primitive forms anyway. I had been called upon to review the menu and strike the right compromise between tasty, sophisticated food and medieval dishes. I had had the same kind of commission at other castles and stately homes. It was an enjoyable way of spending a few days in an unusual environment while being paid for it at the same time.

I had arrived here at the castle in the late afternoon, and after dinner, I had been invited to watch the jousting tournament. It was an exciting spectacle. The brilliant colored flags were now being stirred by some internal mechanism and fluttered bravely as if in a stiff breeze. The magnificent horses snorted and stamped, shaking their gaily decorated manes with pride.

The crowd was thoroughly into the whole thing, shouting and yelling, on their feet as the knights closed in, lances leveled, the horses' hooves thundering and kicking up clods of earth. The lance of the Black Knight—he was the combatant receiving all the boos—missed the helmet of Sir Harry Mountmarchant by inches as the two roared by each other. Sir Harry's lance hit a glancing blow on the side of his opponent's breast armor and the crowd bellowed approval.

The perfectly trained mounts skidded to a standstill, haunches down, hooves churning deep furrows—must be a lot of work for gardeners here, I thought. They turned and stood for a moment, puffing clouds of steam (how did they do that? I wondered). Sir Harry flipped up his visor and looked around for support. It was unnecessary: the crowd was with him one hundred percent. The Black Knight jabbed his lance into the air furiously and the crowd jeered. I presumed that was the medieval equivalent of the digital gesture of derision, deplorably popular in modern sport.

The trumpets chopped the air, clean, sweet sounds calming the crowd's frenzy and alerting the jousting knights into readiness. The horses, superb actors and beautifully rehearsed, pawed the ground, dipped their plumed manes as if eager to engage the enemy, then stood motionless, waiting for the signal.

It was only seconds but it apparently seemed like minutes to the hushed crowd. Just as impatience was about to set in, the trumpets blared, and amid a roar from the assembly, the two riders rocketed their steeds into action. Again, the metallic figures raced at each other and this time both scored hits. Sir Harry half-fell from his saddle; the crowd "ooh'd" loudly until he regained his position with a lithe swing.

Twice more, the spectacle was repeated, until with a shivering crash, Sir Harry hit the Black Knight full on the chest armor and knocked him off his steed. It trotted away and the Black Knight climbed unsteadily to his feet. Cheers of approval went up as the valiant Sir Harry—no man to take advantage of an unhorsed opponent—slid from his saddle and approached the Black Knight, drawing his long broadsword.

The Black Knight looked as if he had recovered now. He drew his own weapon and the two huge swords clashed, with a noise that was amplified electronically amid a shower of glittering sparks, probably generated chemically.

Sir Harry Mountmarchant took a mighty swing, but his opponent ducked and moved, looking for an opportunity. He feinted from the right, then swung backhanded, and a groan of agony came from Sir Harry, cleverly orchestrated by the loudspeakers. He recovered quickly, though, and fought on bravely.

The end came when the Black Knight started a side blow which he switched to an overhead slash. It bounced off Sir Harry's big shoulder guard, whereupon the black-clad villain treacherously pulled a hidden dagger from his belt and attempted to plunge it into Sir Harry's midriff.

This was a move highly unpopular with the partisan crowd, but their fears were unfounded. Sir Harry clamped a hand firmly on the hand holding the blade, pushed the other back, then aimed a prodigious swing of his broadsword at the other's neck.

The clash of metal on metal rang throughout the arena. The Black Knight was rooted to the spot and Sir Harry's blow was powerful and unerring. A crunching, skin-tingling sound could be heard and the shouts from the crowd faded almost instantly as the glittering blade severed the neck of the helmet completely.

Moans of horror trickled into the air and hundreds of eyes watched in helpless fascination. The helmet bounced on the grass and rolled away, leaving a trail of blood behind it.

It finally came to rest upside down, exposing a grisly, gory tangle of flesh that still dripped, running over the black metal and soaking into the soil.

CHAPTER TWO

A_s the crowd watched in stunned horror, four pages ran out, costumed in yellow jackets with blue piped sleeves, baggy blue pants, and ankle boots. They brought a stretcher, loaded the body onto it, and were about to trot away from the arena when one of them pointed to the helmet lying there, still oozing blood. Another page ran back, retrieved it, and stood it on the chest of the deceased. They left the field hurriedly.

Before they had departed, I had already left my seat and gone to the large tent with the scarlet, gold, and black colors of the Harlington family flying over it. One section of it was partitioned off and the pages were removing the body from the stretcher and placing it facedown on a wooden cot. A man came hurrying in. I presumed he was a doctor.

As he approached the body, I witnessed one of the modern improvements to the suit of armor. It had probably taken two or three hours to get a knight of old into, and out of, his armor. But technology had progressed and fitted several quick release clips down the center of the back. The doctor snapped these open quickly and the metal suit opened up like a clamshell, coming apart in two halves.

I was not prepared for what happened next and received one of the biggest shocks of my life as a tiny figure came to life, rolled sideways out of the armor suit, and leaped out. I leaped too, and he saw me and laughed.

He was a dwarf, not much over four feet high, and the face

was that of a fifty-year-old man. He was as agile as a circus performer and I realized that was exactly what he was.

"Scared you, didn't I?" he chuckled in a voice like that of a character in an animated cartoon. "Thought Sir Harry had knocked my bloody head off, didn't you?"

I was recovering slowly. "Your head was bloody," I conceded. "Bloody, convincing, and bloody convincing. How many times a day do you have it knocked off?"

He chuckled in a fair imitation of Donald Duck. "Only once most days, but when Henrik has been on the bottle, I have to take his fall too. He's the other dwarf around here," he added contemptuously. "We've got a few midgets but they can't do this kind of work."

He had powerful shoulders for his height and strong arms that were normal length. His head too was normal, while the rest of him was undersized. He had the face of a person who has endured some very hard times. It was lined and his skin was coarse. His eyes glittered with, well, perhaps not hatred of the world but certainly contempt for it. "I'm Eddie," he said. He sat on the edge of the cot and pulled off his boots. He wore only a gray singlet and gray pants.

"I thought that was a doctor come to confirm that you were dead." I had just noticed that the man had left the tent after releasing the dwarf from his metal container.

"Don McCartney, Entertainments Director. Everybody gets to do all kinds of jobs in this show."

"Must be hot in that suit," I commiserated.

"Midsummer it's like an oven in there. Not too bad today." He gave me a glare of suspicion. "Who are you? Don't allow strangers back here during a performance."

"I advise on foods. I set up the menus when this place first started and now the Harlingtons want them changed, bit more medieval."

He grunted, no longer interested.

"How do you see inside there?" I asked him.

"A visor in the chest, see?" He demonstrated, opening it. I fingered the suit. "It looks so heavy, yet it's so light."

"Heavy enough when you're in it. Made of aluminum; they treat it to look like steel."

"It's evidently strong enough to resist a lance hitting it at the combined speed of two horses—and that must be nearly a hundred miles an hour. A wonder it doesn't go right through you."

He grinned, pleased to be able to expose a few secrets. "The tip is rubber and the lances are sprung."

"Sprung?"

"Yes, there's a spring inside them that cushions the shock. The lance squeezes into itself, like one of the old telescopes. You don't notice that in all the excitement."

"It's exciting all right. You had that crowd breathless."

He smiled proudly. "We put on a good show. Best in the country, lots say."

"Even the helmet, with what I thought was your head inside it, rolled away very convincingly. Ended up with the gory end exposed, too."

"Helmet's weighted at the top to make it do that. Leave nothing to chance, that's our motto."

The man I had thought to be a doctor came back into the tent. "Don McCartney," he said. "I know who you are. Saw you when you arrived yesterday. Sorry I had to rush out just now but we had a problem with one of the horses."

"Horses get better attention than we do," grumbled Eddie, but he was apparently not as callous in that direction as he pretended as he went on, "Not Primrose, is it?"

"She's his favorite," grinned McCartney.

"No she's not," Eddie retorted hotly. "She's the only horse that doesn't step on me when Sir Harry knocks me off."

"None of them step on you. You're too small."

Eddie snorted, made a mock fist at McCartney, and swaggered

out. McCartney watched him go. He was late middle-aged, with the bearing of a military man.

"Have to take care of the horses too, do you?" I asked.

"I spent twenty-five years in the Guards, in the cavalry," he said, confirming my guess. "So I know a bit about horses. Primrose had a limp when she came off after this show but she's okay. Just a momentary strain. Happens often."

He had a strong face and a firm jaw. "Must be an interesting job," I said to draw him out more.

"When I was with the Guards, we had a photographic unit attached to us for a while. We made some training films, couple of recruiting films too. When the film studio at Elmtree wanted to use a couple of our squadrons, I got assigned to liaison.

"We worked out a few stunts, you know the kind of thing—men shot by arrows, falling off horses. The horses needed training as much as the men. When I retired, I heard about a job going here. Did some stunt work at first, then got promoted to this."

"You do a fine job," I said. "I was convinced that the Black Knight would need his head sewed on for tomorrow's performance."

"Took us a while to work out that trick." McCartney smiled.

"You must get the occasional fainter in the crowd when that head rolls."

"Very occasional—and not only women." He picked up the discarded portions of the suit of armor and hung them on a wall rack. "Haven't been able to teach those two dwarfs to keep the dressing room tidy," he complained. Turning to me, he asked, "Going to be around long?"

"Just a few days. I'm working on revising the menus, as you know. We're going to start introducing some of the new dishes right away, then add a few more. It may mean working with some new suppliers in the case of foods you haven't served before. Might take a little time to get them acquainted with exactly what we want. We'll be putting on some medieval banquets for special events. Then there's the kitchens, they'll be called on to cook some dishes that are new to them."

"Not going to get too revolutionary, are you?" he asked, smiling.

"Oh, no. There won't be any elephant ears or larks' tongues."

From another part of the tent, voices were being raised. I saw McCartney frown. The voices subsided. "That's good to hear," he continued. "The customers have enjoyed the food, although I know the committee has decided that we could bring in more people if we offered some interesting old foods, well, new foods which at the same time were—you know what I mean—traditional."

"That's right. Previously, the food was different but not excitingly so. Now we want to really get people interested in eating what people ate in the Middle Ages. But we're bringing it up to date by making use of modern knowledge of tastes and flavors."

"I suppose that's what Miss Felicity had in mind when she started the Plantation," McCartney said.

"I saw the Plantation when I was given a tour, oh, ten years ago, when this whole idea was being put into practice. It had only just been planted then and I haven't had the chance to visit it this time."

"Oh, you will. She'll be anxious to have you make more use of it."

The voices came again. They were more strident now but I couldn't make out any words. I saw McCartney's eyes flicker in that direction. Was it some recurrent discipline problem? I wondered.

They grew yet louder and reached the point where McCartney could hardly ignore them any longer. "You'll have to excuse me," he said. "May be something that needs my attention." He was about to walk out when a flap in the section of the tent separating it from the rest opened.

A skinny young man with close-cropped hair came halfway through. "You'd better come, Mr. McCartney." His voice was tense. "Kenny's ill."

McCartney was curt. "Ill? What do you mean, ill?"

"He's in real agony, Mr. McCartney," the young man said nervously. He wiped his nose on his sleeve. "You'd better come look at him."

He withdrew, holding the flap open, and McCartney hesitated, frowned, then followed him. I went along too. McCartney threw a glance at me over his shoulder and I expected him to tell me to stay there, but he said nothing.

We hurried through a tent section with portable racks full of costumes and shelves heaped with boots, hats, leggings. Through another flap, and we were in a section similar to the one we had just left. Parts of a suit of armor lay on the floor and I recognized it from the scarlet, black, and gold emblem on the breastplate as having been that worn by Sir Harry Mountmarchant in the jousting tournament.

That was secondary, though. Loud moans were coming from a cot where a young man was writhing in pain. His face was bathed in sweat and his hooked fingers clutched his abdomen. In a sudden paroxysm, his body jerked clean off the cot, then subsided. He wriggled and twisted, now trying to hold one knee which was obviously hurting him, then sagged as if utterly exhausted. His breathing was deep and harrowing. His eyes gazed unfocused.

"What's the matter with him?" McCartney demanded roughly.

"I don't know. He's been like this since he came off the field."

McCartney looked down at the figure on the cot. The young man was less active now, just twitching spasmodically, seemingly worn out. He still moaned, though, and was trying to mutter something.

McCartney was frowning. "What the devil was he doing on the field?" he wanted to know.

"He was Sir Harry."

McCartney's face was like thunder. "It was supposed to be Mr. Richard out there."

"I know," said the hapless young man who was caught in the

crossfire. "But he wanted to go into the village and he got Kenny to replace him."

McCartney glared at him. For a moment, he appeared more concerned with a breach of rules than with Kenny's condition. "Have you called Dr. Emery?" he asked.

"He's on his way."

"I have some first-aid experience," I said. "Let me look at him."

I didn't wait for an answer. Kenny's pulse was slow and faint. His breathing was heavy, deep, and irregular. I pulled up one eyelid. The pupil was contracted. As I allowed the eyelid to close, I was aware of an odor in one of the exhalations. It was not a familiar odor but I had the feeling that it had some similarities . . . but to what? I could not make any identification and, anyway, the important thing right now was to maintain his body temperature, which was low.

"Get a blanket," I ordered. "Keep him warm."

The young man hurried out and was back immediately with an army blanket, which he threw over the still-convulsing body. McCartney stared down at the face on the cot.

A voice called out, questioning. "It's Dr. Emery," said the young man eagerly. "I'll get him."

The doctor was gray-haired and gray-mustached, calm and brisk in manner. He took Kenny's pulse, looked at his eyes and his tongue, measured his blood pressure, then put a stethoscope on his chest.

His face gave away nothing but his voice was grave as he said, "I'll phone for an ambulance. He needs hospital attention." He was feeling inside his bag and pulled out a syringe and a vial just as McCartney asked, "Anything you can do for him, Doctor?"

The injection seemed to calm the breathing, and it eased the twitching, but all color had left the face that was still beaded in perspiration. The doctor hurried out.

"We don't have a doctor here but Dr. Emery is on call from the village at all times," McCartney explained. He seemed to want to talk. "I still don't understand why Kenny replaced Richard Harlington."

"He wanted to go into the village," I suggested. "Something urgent probably."

McCartney made an dismissive sound. "Went in to see that girl more likely."

"He has a girl in the village?"

"Yes. Sir Gerald has tried to break it up, even forbade Richard from seeing her, but it doesn't do any good. He slips away at every opportunity."

"Kenny is a regular substitute as Sir Harry?"

"We have three of them play Sir Harry—Richard, Kenny, and another stuntman, Frank Morgan."

"Isn't it a bit unusual to have a lord's son doing a dangerous job like that?" I asked bluntly.

"It really isn't dangerous. It's choreographed to the tiniest move. Anyway, Sir Gerald has tried to get Richard to stop, but he's a headstrong, reckless young man and won't listen."

He looked down at Kenny. "His breathing is slowing, isn't it?"

"Yes, but that might be the doctor's injection, slowing down his body systems."

"What's wrong with him, do you think?"

I hesitated before answering. It made him look at me abruptly. "What is it? Do you know?"

I still hesitated, then I said, "He has all the symptoms of having being poisoned."

CHAPTER THREE

Kenny died an hour after reaching the hospital. Don McCartney was in the breakfast room of the castle early and met me with the news. He was with two others at one end of a table. He left them and motioned me to join him at the other end.

"We don't have to tell you that we are discussing ways to keep as much of a lid on this as possible," he said to me.

I nodded. "I can understand that."

"The Hertfordshire police are sending some people," McCartney said. He looked haggard, probably from lack of sleep. He rubbed a hand over his face. "I didn't get much sleep last night," he said, confirming my guess. "The hospital called about one this morning to say Kenny had died an hour earlier. They said they had finally been obliged to terminate all efforts at resuscitation."

"Did they say anything about the cause of death?" I asked.

"No," McCartney said flatly. He glanced at the others, then turned back to me. "Look, we might as well get this into the open now. It'll have to come out when the police interrogate us anyway."

"What's that?" I had a pretty good idea what was coming.

"You said last night that Kenny had all the symptoms of having been poisoned."

The table was quiet. McCartney regarded me quietly and expectantly.

"I don't know how many people have been briefed on who I am and why I'm here—" I began and Don McCartney waved a hand.

"Nearly everybody at the castle knows. We don't like to have unidentified strangers wandering around."

"You have a lot of people working here," I continued. "I didn't know how far my job had been broadcast. So then you know that my business is food. I'm here to readjust the menus so as to make them more authentically medieval and more enjoyable. I get jobs like this and, once in a while, complications set in."

"Complications?" McCartney said sharply.

"Food has become a very big business. Look at the popularity of restaurants, see how many books, magazines, and television programs there are about food, and consider how much more important a part of our lives it has become. When something becomes that important, lots of money gets to be involved. Rewards are high, motives are strong."

"So you've run across cases of poisoning before?"

"One or two. I know what the most common symptoms of poisoning are and Kenny's seemed to fit in."

McCartney sat back in his seat. "That's a relief."

"Is it?" I asked. "Maybe it suggests something more sinister."

"You mean Kenny was deliberately poisoned?" McCartney was openly skeptical.

"Richard was supposed to be Sir Harry last night. At the last minute, he decided he had to go to the village and see his girlfriend. Kenny replaced him."

"So are you saying that someone wanted to poison Richard?" McCartney rephrased his question.

I shook my head. "I'm not saying anything till the police get here, and then I'm going to be careful."

"That's wise," McCartney said. "The first thing we need to know is what the official cause of death was. After we get that, it may be time for theorizing. I understand that a police inspector called Devlin is coming."

"Know him?"

He shook his head. "We get the occasional pickpocket and a rare break-in," he explained. "They give us extra security for some

special events too, so we talk to various members of the Hertfordshire police, but we don't know this one." He stood up to
go. "I'll let you get on with your breakfast," he said. "I suppose
you might as well carry on as if everything was normal."

He left. I had a half grapefruit, wheat cereal with a banana,
and coffee. I headed for the kitchen but I had only gone as far as
the main dining room when a servant in uniform accosted me.

"Have you had breakfast, sir?" he asked and I said that I had.

"Sir Gerald sends his regards and asks if you could spare him
a few moments."

Very civilized of him, I thought, and considerably more polite
than a Sir Gerald of medieval days would have been in ordering
me to appear before him.

"Certainly," I said. "When does he propose?"

"Would right now be convenient?"

"That would be very convenient," I replied. "Where do I
find him?"

"If you'll just follow me, sir, I'll take you to him."

He conducted me up a long stone staircase with plain iron bal-
usters, curved outward so as to accommodate ladies' crinolines.
On the first landing hung a large framed photograph of Queen
Victoria at the time of the first Jubilee and a large oil of an ancestor, a duke. He was in military uniform, the painting in a
beautiful rococo frame. On the next landing, we went along a
carpeted corridor lined with early watercolors depicting the
grounds of the castle in the eighteenth century. On one side,
mullioned windows gave a view of huge bushes of laurel and
groves of beech trees.

Sir Gerald was in his sitting room. It was a private room adjoining his bedroom and obviously served as a study. He sat at a
wooden desk strewn with papers and books and illuminated by a
large, elaborate bronze lamp. Lamps on the mahogany-paneled
walls cast pools of orange light onto the Chinese carpet, too old

to identify. Family photos, many black and white and some sepia, adorned the walls.

He was wearing a sky blue shirt and a pair of light gray flannel slacks. I had expected a dressing gown or at least a silk cravat. He greeted me cordially, we shook hands, and he invited me to sit.

"I had planned on talking to you this morning but I had not anticipated that it would be under these circumstances," he said. His voice was light but it had a (largely concealed) ring of the aristocracy. I had not met him when I had arrived yesterday nor during the meeting when my mission had been discussed a week earlier. I recalled talking to him a couple of times during my visits years earlier and he did not look any different. He looked some- what like the late Duke of Windsor, I thought.

"Yes," I said. "I watched the joust yesterday evening and was one of the first into the tent to see what medical science proposed to do about the Black Knight's head. I almost jumped out my skin when Eddie popped out. I was talking to Don McCartney when he was told about Kenny being ill. I went with him to see Kenny and was there until the ambulance came."

"A sad business," said Sir Gerald. From what I knew of him, he cared about every man and woman who worked on the estate. The death of one of them would hit him hard. "Hopefully, we'll learn more of the circumstances when the police arrive. I under- stand we can expect them at any moment."

"So I believe," I said politely.

He leaned back. "I wanted to talk to you before they came," he said. "This is why—it's about my son, Richard. I suppose you've heard by now, he should have been in the joust." He gave a wan smile. "We're a tight community here. Word gets around."

I nodded.

"Kenny replaced him," he went on. "What this has to do with Kenny's death I don't know, but I'd like you to see what you can find out. Oh, I know you're here on the other business, but that's all right. You can do that too. It's a good cover."

He looked at me expectantly. "You will do it, won't you?"

"I'm not really a detective," I told him. It was an explanation that I seemed to have to make often. "I don't have a license, I'm not—"

"I know, I know. I've made some inquiries. You did a fine job for Desmond Lansdown. He recommends you very strongly."

"Ah, yes. He asked me to go to Italy and pick a chef for his new restaurant. Some difficulties arose . . ."

"A man was murdered, I understand," Sir Gerald said.

"Well, yes," I murmured.

"Desmond and I belong to the same club."

Desmond is a blabbermouth, I was tempted to say but didn't. Instead, I said, "On that occasion in Italy, I was able to help the police apprehend the criminal." That sounded like the right terminology. "But we don't know that we have a crime or a criminal in this case," I continued.

"In that case, your task will be easy," Sir Gerald countered smoothly. "You will be able to earn double your fee with little additional effort."

"Double?"

"Yes. I am prepared to double your fee if you will undertake this task for me."

I was already contracted to do the menu thing for a fee that was agreed at a level higher than I had hoped. Now it was going to be doubled! Greedy, I warned myself, greedy. At the mention of money, you start to salivate. You should only do that at the sight of a plump roast pheasant, browned to perfection . . .

Sir Gerald started to turn the screw. "I have four children. You will meet them all if you haven't already. Two boys and two girls. Richard is the eldest. He's a headstrong boy and gets into trouble easily. Oh, never any serious problems, but there's a girl in the village he's taken a fancy to—she's the one he was with last night when he should have been in the arena." He paused and smiled wryly. "I say, 'should have been in the arena.' I have tried to dissuade him time and time again from risking life and limb that way, but he finds it exhilarating. Perhaps at that age, I would have too. If I remember correctly, with me it was ballooning."

"I was getting the impression that the joust is not that dangerous," I said. "Steel in the right places, aluminum everywhere else. Spring-loaded lances, highly trained horses, thoroughly rehearsed—the risk seems to have been taken out of it."

"We've done as much as we can. In fact, we've done a lot. It's probably the most spectacular and realistic show of its kind in Europe. We've never had an accident." He stopped and smiled. "Oh, as you get older, you get more timid, I know. Slender as the risk is, I worry about Richard out there."

"In this case, he wasn't out there." I was determined not to be too compliant.

He waved a hand. "All I ask is that you stay around for a few days, stretch out your task with the food if you have to. The business with Richard probably has nothing to do with Kenny's death." His voice took on a harder tone. "I believe you told Don McCartney that you thought Kenny had been poisoned?"

Served me right for thinking Desmond Lansdown a blabbermouth. The pot has no right to criticize the color of the kettle. "He did appear to have many of the symptoms," I began to say.

"There you are then. Another perfectly valid reason to have you keeping an extra sharp eye. We don't want any fingers pointed at our cooking, do we?"

He had me, fair and square. I could even justify myself accepting a doubling of my fee. I had to ask, though, and this was the best time to ask it.

"Sir Gerald, there isn't anything else I should know, is there? About Richard, about Kenny, about anyone else? About the circumstances of Kenny's death? Or anything else here at the castle?"

Was there just the slightest flicker of hesitation? Maybe it was just a natural caution in answering that would be typical of a man of breeding and background. In either case, I didn't have the chance to decide because there was a discreet tap at the door. Sir Gerald called out, the door opened, and the uniformed servant who had conducted me here poked his head inside.

"Pardon me, Sir Gerald. The inspector from the police is here."

CHAPTER FOUR

The north wing of Harlington Castle was, I learned, the least used portion of the edifice. All of the other parts were in active use at all times, but the north wing had not been fully restored and the rooms in it were either empty or used as storerooms. One large room, with full-length windows looking out onto extensive flower beds, had been quickly converted into a temporary operations office for the police.

Due to the large number of people they would want to interview, it was more practical to do it here than keep driving them to police headquarters in the city of Hertford. From the point of view of the people at the castle, this was preferable anyway as it minimized disruption to the routine.

The public announcement system normally operated separately in the various segments of the castle and its grounds, but now it was universal and calls were being put out for groups and for individuals to present themselves at the police operations room.

Sir Gerald's status gained him preferential treatment and he didn't have to suffer the indignity of being brought in for questioning along with the common herd. "You'd better stay," he said. "The police will want to know what you're doing here and it might go down better if I explain."

It was not that Sir Gerald appeared to be the kind who would seek better treatment, though. His manner was affable and friendly, with no trace of condescension. I noticed that he spoke to servants in the same aimiable fashion.

We heard footsteps and a muffled exchange of words outside before the long arm of the law entered.

"Inspector Devlin, Hertfordshire Police." Sir Gerald greeted the inspector and introduced me. Sir Gerald invited us to sit and we did so. Inspector Devlin had a long, gaunt face. It was the face of one who has witnessed many crimes and misdemeanors, not to mention all of the sins to which flesh is said to be heir. The head of unabashed gray hair verged on the untidy. The eyes suggested that their owner was not going to believe a single word you said. The tall, ungainly body sat in the comfortable chair uneasily, rest-lessly, as if eager to be out of there, solving crimes and bringing villains to book.

She was a very daunting figure.

She started in a minor key. Her voice grated and she spoke in long bursts, swiftly as if wanting to get the whole interview over with, but it seemed likely that that was a false impression. She was probably a bulldog when she got her teeth into something. I hoped it wouldn't be me.

"I am aware, Sir Gerald, that you were not directly involved in this distressing event. I will be talking to those who were"— she didn't glance in my direction so I didn't know if she was aware that included me—"but I wanted to speak to you first."

"I appreciate that, Inspector." Sir Gerald put a slight additional polish on his already formidable facade. He managed to amplify his position as master of the manor merely by the lordly way he sat relaxed behind his large desk. "If there is anything that can be done to facilitate your task here, please be assured that every effort will be made to do it. I hope you will not hesitate to come to me if you have any problem, no matter what it is."

"I won't hesitate," said Inspector Devlin, and her gritty tone emphasized her intention to do just that. "Now perhaps you can outline for me—just what happened as you know it."

Sir Gerald did so, briefly and succinctly. The inspector nodded sharply and her eyes swiveled to me. "And this gentleman?"

"We have been very successful here, I'm pleased to say." Sir

Gerald sounded like the chairman of the board presenting the annual report. "The tours, the exhibits, the entertainments—all have been expanded and improved since we first opened nearly ten years ago. Recently, however, we decided that we have been remiss in one area. People today have become much more aware of food than they used to be, cookbooks are being written by the hundred, food critics are treated like gurus, and television channels devote much attention to the subject. We decided that we needed to present meals that are more in keeping with our theme of the Middle Ages. That is why we called in this gentleman to advise."

He leaned forward to push a card across the desk. The inspector picked it up. It was mine, the one I had presented on arrival. The inspector's eyes glinted. They went from me to the card. I knew what was coming. It had come on previous occasions.

"You're a detective." The inspector might have been accusing me of one of the more beastly of a myriad perversions.

"It's a nickname," I hastened to explain. "The Gourmet Detective. You see, I look for unusual foods, rare spices, exotic recipes, that kind of thing. I advise on specialty foods and cooking methods. Here, it's a matter of bringing the food served in line with the Middle Ages. Well, as far as we can, anyway."

"You have a license?" The voice was still condemning.

"I'm not a private investigator. I'm a sort of food-finder, only in food. Not a detective at all, well, not really." I stopped there. Anything more would make it worse.

She put my card back on Sir Gerald's desk. She did it quickly as if wanting to get rid of it before she became contaminated. "I'll talk to you later," she said. Perhaps the menace in her voice was purely in my imagination.

To Sir Gerald, she said, "I understand that the man who died was a stuntman."

"That's correct."

"In your permanent employ?"

"Yes."

"But he didn't play this role every performance?"

"No. They rotated."

"How many of them?"

"Three. Kenny Bryce, the man who died, Frank Morgan, another stuntman, and my son, Richard."

The inspector digested that for second. Not allowing tact to stand in her way, she said, "You permitted your son to participate in this—contest?"

"It's quite safe." Sir Gerald's tone tightened. "We take every precaution. No one has ever been hurt."

"Until now."

"This didn't happen during the contest. It was—something else."

"But your son was supposed to play Sir Harry at this performance, wasn't he?"

For the short time she had been here, Inspector Devlin had gathered a lot of facts.

"Yes, he was," Sir Gerald admitted.

"And why didn't he?"

Sir Gerald was keeping up his front well. Even the formidable inspector didn't faze him. "He had an appointment with a person in the village."

"Who?"

"Jean Arkwright."

"Girlfriend?"

Sir Gerald thought about that for a second but simply said, "Yes."

"It must have been a sudden appointment. Didn't your son know that he was in the joust last night?"

"He knew. We have a schedule. I don't know the circumstances. You'll have to ask him."

"Oh, I will," the inspector said with certainty. "The stuntman, Bryce—any reason that you know of for anyone to want to kill him?"

"Kill him!" Sir Gerald looked alarmed, as if this was a new

thought to him. "No, certainly not. Are you saying he was killed?"

"We hope to know very soon," the inspector said imperturbably.

"Was it poison?" Sir Gerald demanded.

The inspector's rawboned face didn't change. "What makes you think that?"

"Well, I . . ." Sir Gerald wasn't used to this kind of frontal encounter. I took pity on him.

"I said he had the symptoms of being poisoned," I interjected.

"Seen a lot of poisonings, have you?"

"One or two. They sort of come with the business I'm in."

"The detective business?"

"No, the food business."

Sir Gerald was striving to get his composure back and regain his normal mien of nobility. He seized the opportunity of this little contretemps. "Is there anything else I can help you with, Inspector? As I said, I'm always at your disposal. I want to see this affair cleared up as quickly as possible."

"Bad for trade, is it?"

Sir Gerald would have flushed if he had been a commoner, but breeding told. "I want to see justice done and the law carried out."

"As do we all." The inspector got to her feet. "Well, that will be enough for the moment, Sir Gerald." She turned to me. "I'll talk to you later. You'd better stay on here at the castle—whether that's your intention or not," she added flatly.

"I'll be here for a few days," I assured her.

She went out without a further word.

Leaving Sir Gerald, I wanted to get on with my job—my original one, namely, the revision of the menus.

The head chef, Victor Gontier, had a French name and looked French, but he told me he had been in Britain since he was twenty years old. He had a sound reputation in the trade and spoke English with no trace of an accent. He was plump and bespectacled, with a smooth, round face.

His assistant head chef, Madeleine Bristow, had come from the prestigious restaurant of Prue Leith in London. Madeleine looked like a jolly farm girl. She had red cheeks and a full face and retained a little of a Lancashire accent. She had attended a cooking school in Manchester, she told me, and that had started her on her career.

There was some obvious friction between the two of them, though it was covered over by the professionalism of both. We sat in the offices belonging to the kitchen. A bookshelf was filled with cookbooks and binders full of recipes. Certificates and diplomas adorned the walls and a large colored photograph showed Victor Gontier in a tall white hat with the other members of the Maître Cuisiniers de France.

I was aware that I had to employ an increased amount of tact on this assignment. No chef likes an outsider coming in to his kitchen to tell him anything. Most well-informed chefs know a little of food in earlier days but it is only a little. Such knowledge as they may have gathered during their studies has been forgotten by the time they reach any level of recognition. Cooking in a top restaurant is a highly competitive occupation today and staying abreast of changing trends and shifting customer demands all their time. Few chefs have much inclination toward history.

"Goose is not a popular bird," Victor said dubiously in response to my opening suggestion. "You seldom see it on a menu these days. One reason is that many people are aware that it has a lot of fat."

"I'm suggesting the Embden goose from Germany. They are not raised for the production of foie gras and they do not have that large fold of skin that the industrial goose has. As you know, that is where they store the fat produced by the force-feeding that is necessary for the swollen livers of foie gras. Consequently, the

Embden goose is ideal for eating and has only a small amount of fat."

Victor looked skeptical. Madeleine said sweetly, "Why don't we come back to that? Cover a few other possibilities first."

"All right." I was prepared for some resistance. "What about mutton? Not so long ago, everybody ate mutton. Properly prepared, it makes a very tasty meal. It's inexpensive and authentically a historical dish."

"That's a possibility," Madeleine said.

"I suppose we could consider it," admitted Victor.

"Of course," I reminded them, "we're not talking about meals that are simply put in front of people. These would be a choice among several other choices."

Victor nodded, a minuscule nod. Madeleine pursed her lips in thought.

"Venison is a dish that surely would be popular." I knew I was on safe ground with this one. "Meat lovers like it and it has the true ring of a medieval dish."

Even Victor perked up. "We have deer on the grounds. The herd is culled periodically and we serve venison then."

"How do you prepare it?"

"As steaks."

"Good," I said. "If there's plenty of it when you cull, we could widen that usage. Stews, sausages, we could perhaps have a barbecue in a pit outside."

This time, Madeleine inclined her head gently. Victor said, "Yes, that's possible."

"Frumenty was the standard accompaniment for venison in the Middle Ages," I said.

Victor looked thoughtful.

"A modern way of making it would be to make a pudding of whole wheat grains with milk, sprinkle in some chopped almonds, and enrich with egg yolks and color with saffron," I suggested.

"We could manage that," he said.

I had assumed that he could. That was not only the way of making frumentry used in the Middle Ages, it was the modern way.

"Then there's bear steaks, ever consider those?" I asked.

"One of the most popular entertainments here is Daniel and his Dancing Bears," Madeleine said heavily. "The children love them, become very attached to them. I don't think we could ask any of the children to eat them."

"They wouldn't be eating any dancing bears. These would be different bears and besides—"

"I know," Madeleine said. "But would you want the job of explaining that to five-year-olds?"

"That's a good point," I conceded. "We'll rule out bear meat. Gamebirds were prominent in medieval days," I went on. "What do you think of pheasant, partridge, and teal?"

Both gave the question consideration. I knew what they were thinking—that such birds meant a lot of extra work in plucking and preparing. "They increase costs," Madeleine commented.

"True," I agreed. "These birds are much less prevalent now than they were in those times. But we would be charging by individual dishes so these could be priced higher."

"We don't want to increase total meal prices," Victor objected.

"We could emphasize the luxury aspect of gamebirds," I said, "and we could offset these higher-priced items with some less expensive ones."

"Such as?" Madeleine wanted to know.

"Rissoles, for instance." I smiled at her. "Being from Lancashire, you'll know about those." Being too young to have had personal experience of rissoles, she would have heard of them at least, I reasoned. They had gone out of style in the past decades but they had been a major factor in Lancashire eating so she must have heard her parents mention them.

She didn't respond at once. I didn't want to put her in a position of having to admit ignorance so I went on as smoothly as I could, "You're thinking how we could modernize them. I think the best way would be to roll out puff pastry very thin, cut rounds about three inches in diameter, put spiced ground meat into the center, double them over, and deep-fry quickly."

"Like a samosa," said Victor in a voice of explaining the obvious.

"Exactly. They are cheap, very tasty and—"

"We could use beef, pork, or lamb," Madeleine said. She knew when to get on the bandwagon. "We could make variants on them, different shapes, different sizes."

"Excellent idea," I said enthusiastically. "Perhaps even some designs."

"They used to like to offer pastries and jellies in the shapes of animals, flowers, and so on, didn't they?" she asked.

We soon had a few trial menus roughed out and a schedule for introducing them into the routine. When I left them, I felt I had made a good start. After another visit or two, they would be more cooperative. Both were too professional not to be challenged in the kitchen.

CHAPTER FIVE

I was walking across the grass sward when a voice called and out of the corner of my eye I saw a hand waving. A young man and a young woman approached. I didn't need to guess who the man was. A younger version of his father, Lord Harlington, he had exactly the same facial features, although the eyes and the mouth were a little more haughty and verging on the supercilious. The trappings of aristocracy sat on his shoulders more blatantly than in his father's case, but he looked to be in his late thirties so perhaps age would temper the pride.

His sister, Felicity, was two or three years younger, a smooth-complexioned English beauty with corn gold hair. Not as lofty as her brother, there was an air of confidence about her that betrayed money and position.

"Been wanting to meet you," said Richard after introductions were exchanged. "Father told me about your little chat with him. It's good to know you'll be staying on to help us." He shuddered. "Just came from our 'interview' with that terrible inspector woman."

Felicity smiled. It was partly a humorous smile but there was a touch of disdain in it too, which was reflected when she said to Richard, "Serves you right, running off into the village like that. You wanted to do this jousting thing. You argued and bullied and cajoled your way into it. Then what did you do? You went off to meet your girlfriend. And left poor Kenny to be killed."

Richard flushed. "I didn't leave him to be killed at all. I knew nothing about any possible danger—how could I? I'm sick of being told Kenny's death was my fault."

The family argument might shed a few clues if it went on but I didn't want them to get too heated. Better to keep them talking. So I intervened. "You had a regular schedule, didn't you, for when you played Sir Harry?"

"Of course," he almost snapped.

"Had this happened before? You were scheduled but Kenny took over?"

"Two, three months ago," he said sullenly.

"In this case, did anybody know about it?"

He shook his head. "Only Eddie. I couldn't find Kenny, so I told Eddie to tell him he was to go on instead of me."

"Richard obviously had no idea of what was to happen," Felicity cut in, apparently feeling it was the right moment to show some family solidarity. "He's right, he really wasn't to blame in any way."

"Did you eat anything before going to the village?"

He looked at me in surprise. "No. I usually ate a salad before jousting, but not that day."

Felicity was regarding me intently. "You said something about Kenny being poisoned, I heard."

She must have her ear to the ground—the castle grounds anyway. Richard was frowning. Maybe this was news to him.

"I was with Don McCartney when he was told about Kenny feeling ill. I went with him to see Kenny," I explained. "I made a comment about his exhibiting symptoms of poisoning. Maybe I was out of line."

"What did Dr. Emery say?" Richard asked. "He saw Kenny before he was taken to hospital."

"The doctor didn't venture any opinions, and quite rightly. I should have done the same."

"Expert on poisoning, are you?" Richard Harlington had a knack of sounding belligerent.

"I'm not an expert," I said levelly, "but I have been involved in cases where poisons were used."

"Anyway," said Felicity, smoothing the troubled waters, "we'll know in a day or two what was really the cause of Kenny's death."

I returned to Richard. "So only Eddie knew that Kenny was to replace you?"

"As it happened, yes. Eddie was the only one I spoke to and the only one who saw me—and he always helped me dress."

"It only takes one to get you into that armor?"

"It's mostly made of aluminum and very light. It's cleverly designed with clips and spring buckles. It's quite easy to put on."

"Surely it's more important what happened before that," said Felicity. "If Kenny was poisoned, it could have happened earlier."

"It depends on the poison," I said. "Some are nearly instantaneous; some take hours, others take days or even longer."

"If it was poison," Richard said pointedly.

"Yes," I agreed. "If it was."

We parted. Richard looked glad to get away. Felicity gave me a delightful smile and a wave.

The grass that stretched eastwards from the castle moat was crisp and fresh from the morning dew. Two young men in minstrel costumes passed and gave me a cheery "Good morning!" They were evidently on their way to a rehearsal and both looked resplendent and anachronistic in their dazzling colors. The tight saffron yellow jackets with a single row of wooden buttons had over them shoulder mantles of azure blue, which covered the upper part of the chest and hung to the hips in narrow strips. Cherry red pants ended in brown leather shoes, like slippers with upturned toes. Cloth hats in soft gray material had a large metal emblem, and around the waist, each wore a wide leather belt.

A large well stood near the tents where the jousts took place and the wooden bucket on a rope glistened with drops of water. Clearly, Harlington Castle aimed at authenticity.

Two figures were coming out of one of the tents, one normal-sized and the other unbelievably diminutive. As they came closer, I could see that the smaller of the two was Eddie.

"Too early in the morning for me," he was grumbling. "I'm not at my best till noon time."

"You're never at your best, Eddie," said the other. "Not at noon time and not after." He was in his thirties, strongly built, and had a shock of black hair. He nudged Eddie. "Aren't you going to introduce us, you ill-mannered midget?"

Eddie did so, and I shook hands with Norman, the younger son of Lord and Lady Harlington. He looked nothing like his brother or his father. He did not even have that look of the nobility about him. He seemed to be on good terms with Eddie, however, and the dwarf's less than good temper did not seem to bother him at all.

"Ah, yes, you're the fellow who's going to put the kitchen back three hundred years," Norman said with a grin.

"That's my mission," I agreed, "and I trust it will prove a great advance."

"If it brings more money into the coffers, it will be the advance we're looking for."

"Yes, that's what it's all about, isn't it—money?" Eddie said with a sour face.

"Don't mind our tiny friend here," advised Norman. "He takes a small view of life."

"So would you if you were in my shoes," grunted Eddie.

"You should buy a bigger size. Sheer vanity, that's all it is. Keeping up your image."

The badinage between them was obviously nothing new. Even the weak smile with which Eddie regarded Norman showed no true ill will.

Norman sensed my reaction. "We should have a double act," he grinned. " 'Mirth of the Middle Ages' or 'Cromwell and the King—Laugh Your Head Off.' " He turned back to me. "Police been at you yet?"

"I had an interview with Inspector Devlin," I told him.

"Regular terror, isn't she? Wouldn't want her on my trail, I can tell you. Did you help her with her inquiries?"

"As well as I could," I said. "Not a lot I could tell her."

"It should all become clearer when we know what poor old Kenny died from," Norman said. He seemed to be waiting for some input from me, but I wasn't inclined to stick my neck out again with any comments on poisoning, so I just nodded agreement.

"I've told Richard time and time again that he ought not to be doing the joust," Norman went on, "but he doesn't listen to me. He doesn't listen to anybody, for that matter."

"Except maybe somebody in the village," Eddie muttered darkly.

Norman ignored him and went on, "He could have been killed easily—it should have been him in that suit of armor."

"Everybody thought it was him, I suppose," I remarked lightly.

"Yes," Norman agreed readily, then stopped as he realized where that comment was leading him. He went on quickly, "Still, the lucky son of a gun got away with it that time."

"Let's hope there won't be any other times," I said, keeping innuendo out of my tone.

Norman patted the top of the head that was near his hand. "All right, come on, small stuff, we've got work to do. Must keep the flag flying and the gold flowing into the castle treasury."

I watched them go, arguing good-naturedly. Norman certainly was different from his brother. Did I detect some resentment there? It was understandable if there was some sibling rivalry, but he had seemed genuinely concerned about Richard's lack of caution. When Eddie had referred to Richard's girlfriend in the village, Norman hadn't responded. What did that suggest?

I still had one more member of the family to talk to—the younger sister, Angela. If our paths were not going to cross, I would have to contrive an encounter.

The opportunity came after lunch. I ate in the big staff dining room next to the kitchens. Lunch was also served in the other dining room for guests, but for my present purpose, this was the better place. Now that I had an additional assignment, it was more useful at the moment to get familiar with the staff and the family than the guests.

They ate in shifts and I was with the first shift. At my table were two of the stuntmen, who told me they put on sword fights and did some fancy riding; a young woman who ran the library and kept the archives; and one of the staff from reservations.

It was a competent meal, satisfying and well balanced. First came a salad with artichoke hearts, endives, and tomatoes. It resembled the Arlesienne style and lacked only olives and anchovies to be completely authentic. Following that came a choice of seafood risotto gleaming yellow with saffron, or veal schnitzel, or a mushroom and leek casserole.

No alcohol was served, but there were soft drinks, tea, coffee, and a "Castle Cider." As this was being explained to me, it elicited a few winks and laughs. It was made from apples from the castle's own orchards and, though non-alcoholic, I gathered that alcoholic versions occasionally appeared. I was well aware of the powerful ciders from Somerset, which can have an alcohol content higher than that of most beers. Desserts were passed over by most of the table, though one of the stuntmen had a dish of mixed fruit, berries from the castle's own gardens, shiny blackberries and rich red raspberries.

The room was beginning to thin out as I said casually, "I haven't run across the younger daughter, Angela, yet. Does she come in here?"

The librarian, a West Indian girl with a light brown complexion, smiled. "You haven't met Angela yet? It's amazing she hasn't met you."

One of the stuntmen laughed and said something to the other that seemed to be apropos, but I didn't catch it. The young man from reservations was listening with amusement. "Angela usually comes in about this time when she's around. Generally sits at that table." He nodded to one nearby.

The stuntmen took their leave and so did Lisa, the librarian. I stretched out a cup of coffee with the young clerk, but before I could get him away from the problems of running what he described as a castle, a circus, a museum, a hotel, a restaurant, and a stately home all rolled into one, he broke off. He motioned.

"There she is now. That's Angela."

CHAPTER SIX

She was wearing a flowered dress that would have had made some women look as if they were trying for a country look. But then it would have made some women look casually rural, too. In Angela's case, it made her stand out in the crowd.

Having decided that, I realized that she would stand out in any crowd and that the dress had nothing to do with it. She had large dark eyes that were never still, darting around as if she were afraid of missing something. Her lustrous black hair didn't have the look of having come from a hairdressing salon, but that was probably the look she wanted. Her complexion was smooth and contrasted with her dark hair. She had high cheekbones and a face that was both sensuous and strong at the same time.

She came in with three young men. After making their selections at the buffet, they all sat down at a nearby table, talking excitedly. "Don't know how she does it," said the fellow with me, admiringly. "Different bunch every day."

"A popular girl," I commented. "Friendly." He gave me a pitying look.

"Got to get back to work," he said, rising. "Best of luck."

I drank my coffee slowly. One of the young men stayed only a couple of minutes, then left. Another demolished his pork chop, boiled potatoes, and carrots as if famished, then he too left. The remaining young man ate two large sandwiches as Angela ate a salad. As they rose to go, the young man took her plate and his own and headed for the disposal. I seized my chance.

I introduced myself as I materialized at her side. She gave me a smile that was both gentle and inviting. "Oh, yes, you're helping us with the medieval menu idea, aren't you?" she said. Her voice was soft and had an undertone of intimacy that seemed wholly natural and without artifice.

"That's right. I'm also the one who happened to be on hand when Kenny died."

Her dark eyes clouded. "Wasn't that terrible? Do the police know yet what he died from? They seem to be swarming all over the castle."

"If they do, they haven't told anyone here, as far as I know."

"You were there when he was brought in, weren't you?"

"I came in immediately afterwards. I saw the joust, then went into the tent to see if the Black Knight could possibly exist without a head."

Her mouth crinkled in a slight smile. "Yes, they do that very well, don't they? But what happened then?"

It occurred to me that she was asking all the questions and I had read enough mystery stories to know that was not how it should work. I ought to be asking the questions. But the appealing face was turned up to me, and I told myself I could be patient and wait for my turn.

"Don McCartney helped release Eddie from his armor, then he went out. I was talking to Eddie when McCartney came back in. We talked for a few minutes, then we heard loud voices nearby. A young man came in and said Kenny was ill. McCartney and I went to him. The young man said Dr. Emery had been called and he arrived a few minutes later. He had Kenny taken to the hospital, and that's all I know." I hoped I implied that was the end of my role answering questions, but she was too quick for me.

"Didn't someone say it might be food poisoning?"

I decided to adhere very strictly to the truth—very strictly. "I didn't hear anyone say anything about food poisoning."

"H'm," she said as she mentally prepared another question. This time, I got in first.

"It seems unlikely, though, doesn't it? No one else has complained. How could Kenny be the only one to be poisoned by food?"

We were walking out of the cafeteria and into the open air by this time. The same weird mixture of people was walking in various directions. Some wore business clothes; one man had on a carpenter's apron; a brown-robed monk strode by, and three girls in long dresses with bright colored lacing and puffed sleeves were arguing cheerfully.

Angela said nothing for a few paces, but when she spoke it was in a reflective tone. "Have you seen our Plantation?" She was back to the questions.

"Not yet. I want to see it, though. I might get some ideas there for medievalizing the menu."

She did not reply immediately. She was looking straight ahead and seemed to be weighing her words. "It was Felicity's concept, you know. She loves growing things."

Her tone of voice as she said the last words prompted me to say, "And you don't?"

"Ugh," she said expressively, wrinkling her nose. "All that rurality . . . horrible."

"I thought you were raised here among all this pastoral beauty."

"Not me. I'm a city girl."

"But you live here."

She gave the slightest of shrugs. "I'm old enough to leave if I don't like it. Is that what you mean?" A cooler edge was creeping in by the time she reached the end of the sentence.

I was composing a placatory answer when she smiled, giving a wave to a young man in a page's uniform. "Well, maybe I will, one of these days," she said. She sounded as if she meant it, had already been doing some thinking along those lines.

We were still walking and seemed to have strayed some way from the castle. Pathways ran in and out of the clusters of shrubs and bushes, and the gardening bill alone must have run into an awful lot of money. A little further and the castle was out of sight.

"It has just occurred to me that I don't know where we're going," I said lightly.

She smiled again, this time a mocking smile that might have a lot of meaning in it. "There's a gazebo out here you ought to see. The story is that the fourth earl proposed to Lady Emmeline in it after he came back wounded from the Battle of Naseby."

"She accepted, I presume?"

"Oh, that's just a legend, in my opinion. I don't think he proposed to her there at all. I think it's where he first made love to her."

"Do the castle archives support your view?" I asked.

"Of course not. The archivist would have been hung by the thumbs for writing anything like that."

"You've studied the life of the Lady Emmeline, I suspect."

She glanced at me keenly. "Yes, I have. What makes you say that?"

"I'll bet you found her to be quite a little minx."

"Why do you think so?"

"She sounds like the sort of young woman that a modern girl might want to pattern herself after."

Angela sighed. "You're right. I suppose I do. Role model— that's what she would be called today, isn't it?"

"I believe so. So is there no kind of saucy detail in your massive library?"

"Hints, that's all. Very disappointing. There are lots of names, though, of people who were around during that time. Sir Robert this, the Earl of Somewhere, and Lord James that. They couldn't all have been tutors or uncles. I'm sure some of them must have been lovers."

The grass was thick underfoot. The trees, huge oaks, were getting closer together, and the air had a lush smell. Occasional bird calls rang out joyously and leaves fluttered down from the heavy branches.

"So you're taking me to this gazebo, are you?" I asked.

She didn't look back at me. "You want to know all you can about the castle, don't you?"

"Certainly, and I can't think of anyone I'd rather learn from."

She took my hand and we went on through what I believe would be called a leafy glade. We were closer together now and our shoulders rubbed. The air was developing some kind of an electric charge, or so it seemed to me when—

"Hello, you two! Whither are you bound?"

The voice came from behind us. In this sylvan setting, I half expected to find a deer-hunting forester with bow and arrow. It was neither. It was Angela's brother, Norman.

"You must be lost," he said, approaching us. "There's nothing but an old gazebo in that direction. I'm sure you weren't going there," he added derisively.

Angela let go of my hand and her eyes had turned frosty.

"My fault," I said. "I asked what was out this way and we got talking about the history of the castle. We just kept walking . . ."

Norman didn't look at me or acknowledge my words. To Angela, he said, "We have a meeting at two with the people from the County Commission. You hadn't forgotten, had you?"

"No. I hadn't forgotten." Angela's answer was toneless.

"Right. Come on then," he said briskly. He took her by the arm and said over his shoulder to me, "You can find your own way back, I'm sure." It was a statement, not a question.

"Oh, I think so," I said. Under the circumstances, I wouldn't have said anything else.

"Straight along that path, then keep to the left when you come to the hedge," he said, pointing. They walked off, with not a glance from either of them.

I followed the path he had indicated, trying to read some meaning into this encounter. Angela was a flirt and maybe more, but she was surely old enough that she didn't need to have her brother watching over her. He acted strangely possessively for a brother, but maybe nobility and family responsibilities placed increased strain on them. Yet she had all the appearance of a strong-minded woman, even a wilful one.

Surely she could have told him she could find her own way to this meeting. If she wanted to stay with me, that is, and I thought she did. Everything up until then suggested that she was enjoying my company, so why did she accede to her brother so readily?

The path went on, with the trees getting even thicker, but I came to the hedge as Norman had directed. It was dense and tall, taller than me, and looked as if it had been there for centuries. No doubt it had, just like the rest of the castle and its grounds. I turned left and reached a clump of undergrowth, ferns and vines matted so solidly as to be impenetrable. I turned right as there was nowhere else to go and found another path with a hedge along both sides. That in turn led to another path, although this one was little wider than a trail and the hedges loomed higher. I turned again and then again. The trail went on, turns and hedges, hedges and turns.

If I hadn't been so preoccupied with thoughts of the bewitching Angela and those dark eyes, which in turn led to bafflement about the relationship of Angela and her brother, I would have realized it sooner. As it was, the doubt dawned slowly and I must have been reluctant to accept it, preferring to return to speculation about Angela. It was when I came to yet another turn that reality hit me hard.

I was lost.

Lost in a maze.

CHAPTER SEVEN

I was still pondering over my escape from the maze as I sat in the 4:35 train to King's Cross. Escape was perhaps a pardonable exaggeration. At first, I began taking what were clearly wrong turns, but I was seething at Norman for sending me in here and myself for not thinking straight. I had eventually remembered the classic advice for escaping from a maze—take only right turns or only left turns. This is surprisingly hard to do as one is convinced of the correct turn and that conviction is often contrary to the classic advice.

The maze was a popular feature of country houses in the Georgian and Victorian eras. When houses were built, a maze was part of the planning. If a house did not have one, it had to be added. A house from those eras without a maze was like a modern home without an indoor toilet. Hampton Court has one of the great mazes of England. When the house and grounds were re-opened after World War II, visitors would be found still trapped inside the maze when the gates were closed for the night. No one was permanently lost, but numerous small boys caused parental tears and anguish before eventual reconciliation.

It had taken me less than ten minutes to find the way out once I had steeled myself to ignore intuition and just follow the rule. True, they were ten minutes of fuming at Norman and thinking of things to do to him in revenge, but after my merciful release from that green captivity I had cooled off and was banishing the last of those base thoughts.

I had not seen anyone back in the castle, but after a shower and a change of clothes, I sought out Inspector Devlin and told her I was going to London on important business, would stay overnight, and be back here in the afternoon.

She was in a room that was probably once a bedroom, but a long time ago. It did not look like one that was used habitually, but there were charts on the wall and tables with piles of papers. Two constables were on phones, talking in subdued voices. Inspector Devlin was in a cubicle formed by Japanese screens. There was a small table, she had a chair, and I had a chair. That was it. The effect desired was probably intimidation. She fixed me with those gimlet eyes.

"I prefer that no one leaves until a few critical points are cleared up," she said.

"I'll be back in twenty-four hours or so and I do have a business to run," I said in my most reasonable voice.

"Is there anyone in London who'll vouch for you?" She made it sound as if anyone with less authority than the Prime Minister did not count. I was ready for the question, though I pretended I had to think for a moment.

"Inspector Ronald Hemingway at Scotland Yard?" I offered, tentatively, as if I were prepared to work my way up through the hierarchy at the Yard and to the Chief Commissioner if Hemingway's name should be insufficient.

It must have been a surprise blow, but she took it well. "Does he know you?"

"Of course. We worked together a while ago. There was a poisoning case, the Circle of Carême. Maybe you heard of it?" I tried not imply the addition of a phrase at the end like "even out here in the boondocks of Hertfordshire."

She did not confirm or deny, but I had no doubt that every detective in the country must have read about the case, either in the daily press or in the detectives' weekly newsletter, or seen the reports on television. It consisted of two spectacular murders, and no sleuth could have been too occupied sleuthing not to know about it.

"What is his extension at the Yard?" she asked.

"Six oh double six," I said as if I called him every day. In fact, I had looked it up before coming to see Inspector Devlin.

She made a pretence of scribbling it down. "Very well. Let me know when you get back tomorrow."

I avoided saying, "Jawohl," gave her a thank-you nod, and departed. So now, here I was, speeding toward London, where we arrived on time and I was back in the hurly-burly of the great city after the comparative tranquility of the Harlington Castle estate, despite all its visitors.

I took the Metropolitan Line to Hammersmith and walked across to King Street, where my local market was crowded with late shoppers. Len, the fishmonger, greeted me with his usual "What is it today then?"

I riposted with my usual "What's fresh today then?"

There was haddock, scallops, langoustines, prawns, monkfish, halibut . . . then Len pointed to a row of swordfish steaks. "Just came in—from the Caribbean. Lovely, they are." I trust Len's advice, so I followed it and picked out a medium-sized steak.

Back in my flat, which is only a few minutes walk from the market and right in Hammersmith, I put on a CD of one of my favorite "cheer-up" pieces of music. An encounter with death can leave one needing that. This time, I picked Georges Enesco's *Romanian Rhapsody*. The surging throb of those massed violins never fails to lift my spirits. I looked at the mail, which was only bills, poured a mild scotch and soda, sat down and let those wild Gypsy fiddlers send their music flowing over me and soaring to the heavens. I made sure that a bottle of Pouilly Fuissé was in the cooler and went into the kitchen.

This was going to be a simple meal. I make polenta periodically, enough to last two or three weeks, so I had some prepared. I cut a few slices and put them in a baking pan with a little butter and some chopped basil, onions, and sun-dried tomato. I put the pan in the top of the oven, set it on grill, put salt and pepper on the swordfish steak, smeared a thin layer of olive oil on both sides, and put it about five inches from the elements. Mixing the sauce was the next step—melting some butter, adding soya sauce, lemon juice, and chopped capers. This does not need cooking, only warming up to temperature, so I let it sit until the fish was part cooked. I steamed some green beans, drained them and sautéed them a few minutes.

All came together at the same time, which was just after I had popped the cork on the Pouilly Fuissé and taken a few analytical sips. It was an excellent meal, even if I say it myself. After the madcap enthusiasm of those forty violins, I accompanied the meal with a selection of Mozart's piano concertos. These were wonderfully melodic and soothing and all thoughts of murder and violence were temporarily excluded.

The District Line Underground had me at Victoria within ten minutes. I don't have a car—the traffic and the parking make it absurd to have one, and though complaints about public transport in London are common, they still do a magnificent job of moving more than a hundred million people a week. From the station, I walked to Horseferry Road, where the twice monthly meeting of P. I. E. would begin in a few minutes.

Meetings have for some years been held in a building that used to belong to the Ministry of the Environment. One of our members worked there and was able to get it for us at a very modest fee. The ministry subsequently moved out to Haywards Heath, presumably because the environment was better out there, and by some bureaucratic omission we were no longer charged for the room. This new low price suited us fine and we continued to use it. Inevitably, some lynx-eyed official will one day discover this and we shall have to express amazement while declining to pay the arrears.

Meanwhile, we still meet in the room where I encountered Ben Beaumont, our genial president, for the first time. I know that presidents are always called genial, but in Ben's case, it was completely appropriate. Beaming, red-faced, and happy, outgoing and never at a loss for a word, he was the ideal man for the job.

The initials P. I. E. confuse a lot of people. Many think we have monthly bake-offs and exchange recipes. In fact, they stand for "Private Investigators Etc." and the group was initially established as a sort of union for that profession. It was effective enough to survive, but eventually membership declined. This was not because there were fewer private investigators—there were more, but many belonged to large operations and didn't feel the need to be part of something. Still, sufficient lone operators remained, and when these began to decline numerically, someone had the bright idea of admitting as members people who were not necessarily detectives but had some connection. We carefully avoided defining "connection."

It worked. We now had writers of private eye novels, editors at major publishers of mysteries, an engineer who made electronic devices for surveillance, and even a few former police detectives. We encouraged the last to let us believe that they intended to become private eyes, and they obliged. One of them even did so.

I chatted with Tom Davidson, who is a marine insurance investigator, and then with Miss Wellworthy. I believe that our secretary is the only person who knows her first name. Every club has to have a "character" and Miss Wellworthy is ours. She fancies herself as a Miss Marple who can spot a conspiracy at a thousand yards. The Hammersmith Town Council is one of the main hatcheries of plots, according to Miss Wellworthy, but their council members do a fine job of keeping her placated without ever a suggestion that they think her a crank.

"I'm not happy with the water supply," she told me in her determined manner.

"It doesn't have a lot of taste," I said.

"That's not what I mean. Do you know how much fluoride is in it?"

"Not precisely," I admitted. "But it's good for the teeth, isn't it?"

"It may be," she said darkly, "but the nervous system! What is it doing to that?"

We discussed this problem for a few minutes and our conversation ended with her assuring me that she was not going to tolerate local government tinkering with the health of the community. I had a couple of minutes to talk to a popular romantic novelist who drops in on us occasionally to ask about the finer points of being a private eye. She feared that the romantic novel had passed its peak and the future lay with romantic suspense, as she called it.

The man I was looking for did not seem to be present and it was time for Ben Beaumont to bring us to order, so we sat and listened to the minutes of the last meeting and a statement by the treasurer. Then followed a reminder that the group was organizing a trip to Edinburgh for a mystery conference, and finally our speaker stepped up. As he did so, I saw the man I had been looking for come in quietly and sit at the back.

Our speaker was Robert Levine, a criminal lawyer. He spoke first on the lawyer-detectives of fiction—Perry Mason, Matthew Hope, Mr. Tutt, Scott Jordan, John J. Malone, Jake Lassiter, Judge Dee, and others. Then he compared the reality where the opportunities for a lawyer to act as a detective were, he said, extremely limited and heavily frowned upon. Lots of questions ensued, and our speaker dealt with them admirably. When we rose afterwards, I was among the first as I wanted to be sure to catch the man I was after.

Edgar Sampson had retired after spending many years as security chief at Millward House in Yorkshire, one of the great country homes in England. A treasure trove of paintings and sculpture, it also possessed a fortune in jewels, gold, and silver. It was a natural target for thieves, and Edgar had a well-deserved reputation for his ingenuity in devising protective measures. After a first retirement from his position at Millward House, he had then become a consultant in security techniques, and he'd been in great demand. He had now retired again and was living a somewhat lonely life since the death of his wife. Clubs like this were a chance to see friendly faces and chat about old times. It was old times that I wanted to talk to him about—particularly at Harlington Castle.

"Yes, sure, I was there a few times," he told me. He was a short, chunky man with a square no-nonsense face that must have comforted many of his clients. "Lord Harlington was a real gent, it was a pleasure to do business with him."

"Any problems?" I asked.

"What's the interest?" Edgar wanted to know, cautious as always.

I told him of the commission to update the food—back to the Middle Ages. He nodded. Food was not high on Edgar's list of priorities. Then I told him of the death, and he looked grim. "Do the police suspect murder?"

"It's a possibility," I said. I could be cautious too. "The critical point is this"—and I proceeded to tell him of the joust that was supposed to feature Richard Harlington and how Kenny came to his death instead.

Edgar stroked his chin. "Never met Richard. He was at Oxford when I went to Harlington Castle. His sister, Felicity, had just come back from school in Switzerland, I remember. A very nice young lady."

"What about the other two children? Were they there? They were younger, maybe they were at school somewhere too."

Edgar frowned. "They only had two children."

"Two? No, they have four."

Edgar shook his head. "Only two."

"That's strange. You're sure?"

Edgar snapped his fingers. "Wait a minute. Now I remember. After my last visit there, Lady Harlington died. He must have married again. The other two must be his second wife's children."

"I did think it unusual that they looked so different," I said. "That must be why. But tell me, Edgar, any crimes during your time? Attempted or successful?"

He paused, clearly running through what must have been an

extensive mental file. "Nothing big," he said finally. "I recall one instance of a fellow who hid in one of the rooms after the last tour had gone through. During the night, he filled a sack with antique silver, then tried to get out. He was an amateur, didn't know that the alarm system worked the same going out as getting in."

"That was all?"

"A couple of other attempts at break-ins through windows. On both occasions, the thieves took off as soon as the alarm sounded."

Edgar gave me a keen look. "So the police think that it could have been an attempt on young Richard's life? Somebody thought he would be in the joust, didn't know that this Kenny would replace him?"

"Nothing to support it so far. It has to be considered, obviously."

"You were there when it happened, you said?"

"Yes, I was."

"So the police want you to stick around."

"Yes. I managed to get twenty-four hours off for good behavior, though, so that I could come here."

"Who's handling the case?"

"Inspector Devlin, Hertfordshire Police."

Edgar shook his head. "Don't believe I ever met him."

"It's a she."

Edgar pulled a face. He was evidently not a supporter of the movement for women's equality, at least not in the realm of law enforcement.

"Anything I can do to help, let me know," he said.

"If I really get into trouble and you have to smuggle a file in to me, make sure it's in a chicken pie, plenty of chicken, well seasoned, crisp crust . . ."

CHAPTER EIGHT

The next morning, a fine drizzle and a gusty wind were the opening salvo in Mother Nature's war on the human race. Rain spattered the window of the train as we rattled and swayed out of Hammersmith Tube station while the smell of wet coats and umbrellas filled the carriage.

The Smithfield Meat Market used to be a vast mausoleum of blood-dripping carcasses, glistening raw rib cages, crimson limbs, and the sickly sweet smell of death. Progress and technology have brought us a sterilized version, all clean and tidy with nothing to offend the eye, nose, or mind.

I made my way through a row of trucks waiting to be loaded and into an office area with wall-to-wall computers. No one paid me much attention and I didn't need any; I knew where Max's office was. Even without that knowledge, he would not have been hard to find, for he was on the phone and his bull-like voice transmitted great distances.

His full name was Max Rittmeister, but everyone knew him as Max the Knife. He had a large bald head and a scar on one cheek that he claimed he had received while dueling as a student in Heidelberg. Another version said he'd inflicted it on himself with a carving knife while drunk, but nobody repeated that version within earshot of Max. He was big and powerfully built. He had been a POW in England during the war after being shot down as a rear gunner in a Dornier bomber. When the war was over, after a brief sojourn in bomb-shattered Germany, he returned to England and resumed his life as a butcher. As long as I had known him, he knew more about the meat business than almost anyone else in London.

He hung up the phone as I came into his office. "Been out of town?" he greeted me. "You only come to see me when you need something."

"Nice to see you again too, Max. No, I haven't been out of town, and yes, I do need something, but it's something that can make you some money."

He grunted his lack of conviction but I knew that was only an act. The mention of making money would have secured his attention. The meat market operates through individual companies which are, in effect, middlemen between the farms and the customers. Max was one of the establishment's three supervisors; he was responsible only to the meat market but had jurisdiction over the quality of the products sold by the companies. It was the responsibility of Max and his associates to maintain standards by exercising semiofficial control over the farms and the companies. In Max's case, that control could not have been more rigorous if it had been fully official.

"Want to look around first?" he asked.

"Not this time," I told him. I went on, "Livingstone Farms are the supplier in this case."

He made a guttural sound that was as near as Max ever got to approval. I knew it meant that they ran a sound operation because if they didn't, Max would already have taken some action.

I outlined the task facing me at Harlington Castle. I knew that although Max was not an expert on the food of the Middle Ages, he had an encyclopedic knowledge of food history in general. He wouldn't make it easy for me, though.

"So what can I tell you? What can I sell you? You want mutton? I can get you mutton."

"We're considering it, but it's not going to be that popular. People think of it as a food nobody wants to eat any more. Roasts of lamb would be good, don't you think?"

Max shrugged. I knew that the challenge would get through to him quickly. "Could be," he said. "Lamb is a reasonable price right now. They used to eat roast lamb with ginger sauce in those days."

"They needed the strong flavor as the meat was often past its prime. Today, I think we can consider less powerful sauces and bring out the flavor of the meat itself."

He nodded as if he couldn't care less. He was getting more interested.

"Parsley sauce, you think?" I prompted him.

"Lovage," said Max. "They used a lot of lovage in meat sauces, sometimes on its own, sometimes with thyme."

I nodded appreciatively. He was coming round. "In a cream base, you mean?"

"Right. Coriander and onion was another popular combination. They added them to a butter and red wine base."

"I was thinking too of some of the vegetables, chopped to provide thickening. That way, they also give a different taste from the more obvious sauces."

"Green beans," said Max at once. "They'd chop them with turmeric and cumin, put them into a stock, then add some breadcrumbs at the end to thicken the sauce even further."

"Good, yes, that would be different," I told him. "What about pork? How are your supplies?"

"The pork from Lancashire is hard to beat right now. Good price, too. Of course, a suckling pig is a nice touch. Now they really look Middle Ages."

"Some plum sauce sharpened up with vinegar would go well with that, wouldn't it?"

"Real good."

"How would you supply us the suckling pig, though? The nearer to final preparation the better, I think. There aren't many cooks at the castle who know the tricks like you do."

"We'd clean through the throat and hang from the neck. We'd

open the skin under the earflaps so you could squeeze the stuffing in that way. You'd need some calf's brains to make the stuffing really authentic . . ."

Max was thoroughly hooked by now. He went on to recommend baked ham as another dish popular in medieval times. "But make sure it's not salted," he cautioned. "They sell you ham loaded with salt today to help preserve it. You want to bring in a salty flavor only through vinegar, fish pickle, and anchovy paste. Never with salt."

An hour later, I had a long list of ideas as well as Max's estimates of prices and quantities. Ever a storehouse of information, he had gone on to veal roasts and a lecture on how a baron of beef should really be prepared. I left, quite sure that the meat side of the medieval banquet problem at least was solved.

For lunch, I stopped in to see an old friend with a restaurant on Kennington Road, near the Oval. When Dick Lewis had opened Harris House, I had been skeptical about its success. He had taken this step after years of running a restaurant on the island of Harris in the Outer Hebrides. It had been very successful, and when the hostile climate of the North Atlantic became too much for him, he took the bold step of moving to London.

Hebridean food was a novelty, I had to admit, when he first opened. Whether it would be popular enough, I doubted, but within a year Dick had proved me wrong. People wanted good, wholesome food, well cooked and nicely served. Dick managed a fine blend of homely dishes made from natural ingredients, all fresh and yet surprisingly piquant. This was the main reason that this particular restaurant had come to mind out of so many—there was a strong parallel between Dick's food and the medieval food at Harlington Castle.

The place was tastefully decorated and had the appearance of a superior and perfectly kept farmhouse. Vases of flowers on the tables enhanced the image.

One of Dick's secrets was that he made fuller use of Oriental spices than one might expect in Hebridean cooking. The cauliflower and fennel soup was fragrant with its seasoning of coriander and cumin, and the ingredient that made all the difference was the crushed dried pomegranate seeds, adding a fruity but firm aftertaste.

He brought a smoked mackerel spread next and two slices of black bread. "Not enough to be called a course," Dick said. He said it so I could enjoy a typically Hebridean plate of scallops in oatmeal. In the Hebrides, scallops are called clams. The biggest and freshest are obtained by diving, which makes them more expensive—but very much better—than the dredged variety. Oatmeal is used in place of breadcrumbs and adds an extra dimension. A pungent accompaniment is tomato sauce with plenty of tamarind.

I was earnestly assimilating all these ideas.

A large percentage of Hebrideans are vegetarian. This originated from necessity as the bitter weather often limited the population's food to what they could grow themselves. But then it became a preferred way of eating for many. Dick offered me a choice of meats, though, starting with venison. Deer are wild in the Hebrides but sparse in number. The popularity comes from the fact that it freezes better than any other meat.

Lamb features in several dishes on the islands, but as Dick had said to me once, "Kill a lamb when it weighs twenty pounds rather than wait till it grows to eighty pounds—doesn't make sense!" To the thrifty Hebrideans, battling the elements for survival, it made a lot more sense the way Dick put it. "You often hear the comment, 'Mutton dressed as lamb'—well, we serve lamb dressed as mutton," he said.

I settled on a roasted pheasant. The birds were introduced some years ago into the Hebrides but did not do well until plantations were established for them. They are really best when roasted, but I told Dick that would be too much for me for lunch, so he proposed the pot roast.

He confided that this method was usually used so the cook could choose birds too tough for roasting, even though those he could obtain here in London were tender enough. Nevertheless, he was proud of the pot-roasted pheasant. It was cut into pieces and boned, cooked with carrots, onions, and celery, seasoned with bayleaf, thyme, and lemon peel, with some quince jelly added at the end.

Every housewife in the Hebrides has her own way of making scones. Some sweeten with sugar, some with treacle, some use sour milk to lighten the texture. They are known by the names of their originator, so Mary Ann MacSween's scones and Kathleen Morrison's scones are two of the best known. Dick brought me a couple of each when I declined dessert. Golden brown, light but not airy, they tasted as good as they looked.

At the beginning of the meal, I had asked, "They are still not producing wine in the Hebrides?" Dick's answer was inevitable, but he brought me a half bottle of a wine from Hampshire, "only thirty miles from here." It was a sound, light white with a firm finish.

I left Harris House fully satisfied, having assured Dick that his food was better than ever. I also had a headful of notions for augmenting the castle's medieval table.

London's supply of fish in earlier days came from Billingsgate Market, where the turrets of the Tower of London made a splendidly appropriate background. It was a dour Victorian building with spidery iron girders. I remembered my father taking me there when I was at a very young and impressionable age. I recalled the stalls in the bays, the hundreds of porters carrying their impossibly heavy loads, the dead eyes of the fish, the haggling and bargaining that took place before the porters hoisted the dripping wet boxes of purchases out to waiting transport.

Today, much of the fish trade has moved to Docklands, five thousand acres of recently developed land just beyond fabled

Limehouse. The elevated railway gave fine views of it; the sky had now stopped raining and sunshine threatened.

A large warehouselike building was at one end of the road I was looking for, and had a sign: "London Original Fashions." I peered in a side door, but all I could see was row upon row of Asian girls sitting at sewing machines, sewing labels onto garments. Next to it, another warehouse-type structure housed several small vans that were being loaded with leather clothing. I hadn't realized that so much leather was worn or that so many items of the clothing were so skimpy. Then I noticed that one of the vans was stenciled "S and M Specials," so I supposed that explained much.

By the time I reached the end of the row, I had come to the conclusion that this was not the elite part of Docklands. An unpleasant odor was in the air but I could see nothing to account for it. The buildings were not numbered, but the one at the end must be the one I was looking for. "Seven Seas" had been a supplier of fish to Harlington Castle for some time, according to the files, though the name was not known to me. The unpleasant odor increased as I got nearer and there was no doubt that this was the place. A sign proclaimed "Main Entrance," followed with the admonition, "No salesmen, no visitors," which sounded forbidding. I went in.

I was in a small office, one of a row of small offices. The walls were made of glass close to the ceiling, but not for reasons of visibility because they were too dirty to see through. An umbrella stand and a bucket of dead flowers adorned this would-be lobby. I was looking to find my next move when a door opened and a large man entered.

He wore dark blue overalls and stomped loudly in heavy boots. He needed a shave and his hair was short and aggressively bristly. His small eyes regarded me with suspicion. "No salesmen," he growled. "See the sign?"

"I'm not a salesman—"

"No visitors either."

"I'm not a visitor. I want to talk to you about supplies of seafood to Harlington Castle."

The name didn't ring a bell. Even Big Ben would not have penetrated that skull at five yards range. He continued to eye me as if he were trying to decide which limb to break first.

"I'm sure you want to keep on selling us fish," I said with a smile that required a significant effort. "After all," I added, "we are your biggest customer."

I had no idea if that was true but it sounded impressive, and after some seconds, the message reached its mental destination. "Better talk to Violet," he muttered. He motioned through the doorway by which he had entered. "Down the end."

I lost no time hurrying in that direction. Talking to Violet sounded like a vast improvement over that Neanderthal throwback. Talking to any female sounded good to me. The corridor was lined with more offices. Through most of the windows, silhouettes of human forms could be seen and telephone bells rang shrilly.

At the end of the corridor was a figure even larger and more menacing than the one I had just left. He was just as unshaven and his eyes were even smaller.

"I'm looking for Violet," I told him, my eyes roaming in search of a female form.

"Me," he said gruffly.

I stared. My disbelief must have been obvious.

"Dennis Violet. What do you want?"

I explained why I was there. He listened with a lack of reaction that told me nothing about what he was thinking—if he was thinking. "So you see," I wound up my spiel, "I'd like to know what other fish you might be able to supply for us, besides the current ones. Fish that are less common and even unusual. The boats are trawling deeper now than ever before and new species swim into the nets all the time. Some of them are discarded because they are not what the fishermen are going for, but we could have an interest in them at the castle. Save throwing the fish back, and you'd make money from them."

The unpleasant fishy smell was as strong in here as outside. Perhaps it softened the brain, I thought. No signs of intelligent life flickered in the tiny eyes of the man in front of me and my doubts about Seven Seas as a reliable supplier were reinforced. I wanted to knock on his forehead and ask if anyone was home.

"What do you think?" Maybe a direct question would stir some primal response.

"Eels," he said.

I was so surprised, I didn't answer right away. It was a good suggestion and I hastened to tell him so. "Yes, eels—they were very popular in medieval times. Good idea. They'd be even more popular today if only they didn't look like eels." Maybe he had heard that one before; at least it prompted no flicker of acknowledgment.

"What about freshwater fish?" I asked. "We don't seem to have served much in that line at the castle."

"Don't get much of 'em," was the response.

"Tench, pike, carp." I tossed out the names as if throwing out a line but I did not get even a nibble. "Grayling, perch?" The head movement might have been a shake.

"I see from the files that we get oysters from you. They seem to go well but your prices are a little high."

"Getting to be less of 'em," was the comment, and I had to agree.

"That's true. So really your supply is cod, haddock, sole, turbot, and herring?"

"S' right."

"No salmon?"

He shook his head. "Only smoked."

"Scottish?"

He nodded.

"What about tilapia?"

Another shake.

"It's the fish they fed the workers who built the Pyramids. It went out of style for many years, but recently they have been cultivating them in the Caribbean. You see them in Florida more and more."

"Not here," said Dennis Violet.

We chatted a few minutes longer. The input to the conversation was ninety-eight percent to two percent, with me contributing the vast majority. He had little to add and I was getting increasingly skeptical. Dennis began to fidget, clearly anxious to usher me out. I sniffed as I turned to go. "Do you smoke any fish?"

"Not allowed here."

"That smell . . ."

"We burn some rubbish. Heads and tails get in with it sometimes."

I thought that surely that was not allowed either, but he was not a man to pick an argument with. I thanked him and headed down the corridor. He made no attempt to show me out but watched me every step of the way. Outside, the smell was stronger. I walked around the back of the building.

There was a stack of boxes. They carried a stenciled name in Cyrillic lettering and had been shipped from Riga in Latvia. The smell seemed to be a little stronger here and I scrutinized the roof. A strangely shaped conical projection was emitting the very slightest amount of smoke. In the gusty air over the Thames, it was almost unnoticeable, and then only in a rare moment of calm.

I hurried toward the Docklands Light Railway terminal. Seven Seas was buying salmon from the Baltic, where it is significantly cheaper because it is an inferior fish in taste and appearance. They were smoking it illegally and no doubt selling it as prime Scottish smoked salmon. I increased my hurried pace. The staff of Seven Seas would not be gentle or forgiving if they learned that an outsider knew their secret.

CHAPTER NINE

I took the 4:45 train and was back at the castle soon after six. The gates had just closed to the daytime crowds and those attending the evening joust and banquet had not yet started to arrive. I did as I was bid—I reported to Inspector Devlin.

She was in the main hall, talking to two uniformed police, when I located her. She held up a hand to restrain me until she finished, then beckoned me over. I wanted to say something mildly humorous, but after considering various possibilities, I just said, "I'm back, Inspector."

"Ah, the Gourmet Detective. I hope you haven't been detecting."

"I went to a meeting of a club I belong to, then to Smithfield Meat Market, then to a supplier of seafood in Docklands," I said.

She nodded briefly.

"Any progress in the case?" I asked.

"We'll be making a press release tomorrow." So much for being a Gourmet Detective—I was not going to get any special treatment. I took my leave and ran right into Felicity Harlington, who was also leaving.

"Congratulations," I said. "You've succeeded in escaping from the ogre's den too."

She laughed. It suited her classic face. All her features were pleasing.

"It's hard to believe there's any crime in Hertfordshire," she said. "Inspector Devlin must terrify every criminal in the county."

"Let's hope she has the same effect here and can settle this terrible business."

She nodded. "How's your project coming along?" she asked.

"Fair. A couple of things I wanted to ask you, so I'm glad I've run into you."

"Surely. Glad to help."

"I was just about to head for the bar," I said. "Care to join me and I'll tell you what they are?"

"A fine idea." She smiled.

The large bar that adjoined the main dining room was empty except for a couple of drinkers who looked like stuntmen. I hoped they were not on duty this evening. We each ordered a gin and tonic, and I told her of my conversation with Victor Gontier and Madeleine Bristow.

"Discovering consumer reaction to changes is always a tricky job," she admitted. "But I'll do some thinking on it. I know we can come up with something."

"Fine. The other thing is this . . . I know what the menu in the dining room lists, but I'd like to taste the dishes myself. I mean, I know some of them need changing, but I might get some further ideas from eating with the guests."

"You might get some immediate customer reaction too," she commented. "Look, we're not fully booked tonight. Want to eat there? I can give you a pass."

"Great. Are you busy tonight?"

She smiled again, ruefully, I thought. "Can't, I'm afraid. Having dinner in the village with a rep from a travel agency. Another time though?" She declined a second drink and left. I made my way to the kitchen.

Victor Gontier was supervising the preparations for the evening meals. He greeted me without cordiality but politely enough. "I was in London for the day," I told him. "A friend at Smithfield gave me a few good suggestions. Perhaps we can can go through them tomorrow."

"Yes, all right."

"I was also at Seven Seas in Docklands."

He said nothing and his face did not indicate any concern with my statement.

"You've visited them, I presume?" I asked him.

"Some time ago," he said. "Our supplies office places the orders. I have nothing to do with that."

"Who keeps in touch with Seven Seas?"

"I do." He frowned. "Is there something wrong?"

"I don't believe they would pass a routine quality-control inspection," I said. "When were you there last?"

"It was—ah, it must have been a year ago."

"Or more?" I pressed.

"It could have been more—does this have some connection with Kenny being poisoned?" he asked in alarm.

My alarm almost matched his. I didn't want the formidable Inspector Devlin accusing me of meddling in her investigation. She was already suspicious of me, quite without cause—well largely without cause anyway. If she heard that I was spreading a story of poisoning, she'd have me in the castle dungeons by nightfall.

"I went to see the Seven Seas operation to see what other fish they could get for us," I explained. "That's all." He looked relieved. "At present, they seem to be limited to cod, haddock, sole, turbot, and herring," I added.

"That's all we get from them, other than smoked salmon," Gontier said, glad to be on safe ground discussing seafood.

"Is the salmon of acceptable quality?" I asked casually.

"We have never had any complaints."

That was quite possible. An expert can make the poorest fish taste good, thanks to the smoking process. Smoke contains over two hundred components, including dozens of alcohols, acids, and phenols. Most of these influence the flavoring and coloring as well as acting as preservatives.

"Did they have any suggestions for other fish?" Gontier asked.

"Eels was the first suggestion. A good one, too, I thought."

Gontier nodded. "Indeed. Very popular in the past."

"Greatly prized in France," I agreed. "Why don't you start thinking about a few recipes for them? Eels are not unknown in England but we need some ways to conceal their eel-like characteristics, make them less like serpents."

Gontier smiled for the first time. "I will do that."

"Eels were very popular in England at least a thousand years ago," I said, keeping my tone light and conversational so it would not sound as if I were lecturing, "Eel pie was the way most people ate it. They skinned the eels, chopped them into pieces, and simmered them in fish stock. Then they sautéed them in butter, strained in the stock, added cream, and poured the resulting mixture into a pie crust. They were sold on street corners and were an early form of fast food. They continued to be popular until fairly recent years."

"We could try that," Gontier nodded.

As I left, I thought about his responses. He was probably delinquent in not keeping in closer touch with his suppliers, but maybe the pressures of the job here made it difficult. The "supplies office" he mentioned might be worth a visit. Perhaps if the bureaucratic complex of Harlington Castle was handling the purchasing of food as well as everything else, they were too far flung to be efficient.

The banquet hall had high, beamed ceilings and had probably really been the banquet hall in medieval days. Strains of melodious ballads drifted down from the minstrels' gallery, high above the main doorway.

Half a dozen tables had about eight diners at each. A large

silver saltcellar was the centerpiece of each table setting and a jeweled model of a ship contained various spices, all labeled. Two wassail bowls contained wine, one white and one red. We helped ourselves with the silver ladle, though four businessmen opposite me preferred to have the serving wenches do it for them. The girls did it charmingly, having to lean over the table so that their breasts threatened to pop out of their exceedingly low-cut dresses.

A spit turned slowly in the huge fireplace. The large slab of veal on it had already been cooked in the kitchen and the fire was keeping it warm. The smell was rich with the odor of thyme and a hint of garlic. The juices still dropped and sizzled on the hearth.

Torches burned in wrought-iron sconces on the walls and colored candles flickered on the tables. A jester in a colorful costume was going from table to table telling jokes and confiding scandalous secrets about the serving wenches. Loud laughter came from the next table where a group of Asians, probably Koreans, seemed to be enjoying the jokes tremendously, even though they were laughing in all the wrong places.

I was sitting between a Scottish couple, who were a little disconcerted by the whole event, and a travel journalist from South Africa, a young fellow who admitted that he was new at this. We were served soup first. It would have been called a broth, though it had a few vegetables in it. I was listening for comments on it but there were none, which was fair because it was that kind of soup.

Next, the waitresses brought a choice of two fish dishes. One was salted herrings, a popular dish of medieval days and still favored today in Scandinavian countries. I chose the alternative, which was shrimp and pieces of crab in a spicy sauce. The discernible spices were cumin and turmeric, both as popular today as they were when they were essential to covering up shortcomings in the fish or meat. Both of the dishes received comments that were approving but not wildly so. The journalist and I tasted each other's. Across the table, a young couple from Norway were probably on their honeymoon and enjoying everything, especially the herrings.

Trays of miniature appetizers were handed around by the girls. Some were chopped chicken liver on a triangle of toast. These would have been made with cod liver in medieval days. Others were similar, but with a meat paste somewhat similar to deviled ham. That can be a cheap and easy spread and has been known to be a way of getting rid of meat scraps, aided by the use of a hot mustard as yet another coverall. The serving of appetizers after soup and fish was not routine, but came from the custom of offering a dozen or more courses, and the order of these could vary widely. People in those days ate very much more than we do today, and even if they were to pick and choose from among the various dishes, their total intake was still much greater.

The South African was reluctant to be derogatory, but with a little prodding, he confided that the appetizer pasties popular in South Africa were much better, especially the *keeries*—South African for curry. The curried meatballs rolled in pastry were a hit at any function in that country.

Up to now, the food had been so-so. When I had helped set up the menus previously, there had been several dishes that I thought I remembered as being tastier. Certainly, many changes had been made and some of them for money-saving reasons. I made a mental note that these earlier courses would be an ideal place for one of those eel dishes—perhaps the eel pie. Our ancestors had served them with vegetable purées, which should be very acceptable today.

A small sole accompanied by a few boiled potatoes followed. It was served in meunière style—lightly sautéed in butter and lemon. This was universally popular. Then came the main course: the veal roast. It was placed on the table with a flourish by two of the serving girls. It sat on a silver platter and had already been carved into slices. It oozed flavor as the bowls of carrots, green beans, and peas were brought in.

"Shouldn't this be roast beef?" questioned the South African upon learning that the roast was veal.

"Beef was traditional," I answered, "but by no means as common as most people think. The reality was that cattle were working animals. It didn't make economic sense to kill them at the age of ten or twelve in order to eat them when they had another twenty years of work left in them. A further factor was that when they were old, their hide was worth more. It was thicker and stronger as well as bigger, so it brought more money."

"So they ate veal roasts? Like this one?"

"Yes, and pork roasts, too. Pigs have always been a good provider of meat—so much of them can be eaten, right down to the feet and jowls."

I reminded the Scottish couple that in their country, the veal would have been presented with a main side dish of blancmange. Today, this is still popular in England—even though it has declined considerably in recent decades—as a dessert.

It consisted of shredded chicken boiled in milk. Over the centuries, sugar was added, then the chicken was omitted so that it became a dessert. In medieval times, though, blancmange would come with a main course as often as potatoes. It could be considered as an alternate to the frumenty I had mentioned to Victor Gontier as an accompaniment to venison. Both blancmange and frumenty would have been found in middle- or upper-class homes where snobbishness prevailed to the extent of looking down on potatoes as peasant food.

Brown bread was being placed on the table throughout the meal and I made a mental note about that, too. It was an ordinary wheat bread and I thought an improvement was due. Bread made from rye or barley would be good choices—different tastes and textures would be imparted by both.

Trifle was an uninspired dessert. Foreigners unaccustomed to it would enjoy it, but surely English visitors would look for something different and special. This trifle was acceptable—the sponge-cake was fresh, you could just taste the sherry, and the custard was creamy and eggy. On the critical side, it was too sweet, it did not have enough peaches and strawberries (both essential for an authentic trifle), and it had no flavor of brandy. All economy measures, I presumed.

Glasses of foaming mead were brought. No one was really dissatisfied and I had a lot of notes for improvement. We all left happy.

CHAPTER TEN

I breakfasted before most of the guests. Grapefruit juice, an English muffin with marmalade, and coffee were just enough to stave off morning hunger pangs, and I was leaving the dining room when a uniformed constable intercepted me. A number of them were still on the premises. A few seemed to be stationed here but others apparently came in from Hertford as required.

This one was a polite young man. "I wonder if you could accompany me, sir. Just a couple of points . . ." Being interviewed by the redoubtable Inspector Devlin was not the way I would have preferred to start the day, but I was in no position to be selective so I said, "Certainly," and followed him.

To my surprise, he did not head for the main castle buildings. He went in the opposite direction, toward one of the car parking areas. "Where are we going?" I asked. He waved a vague hand. "Just over here, sir."

I examined him as we walked. He certainly looked like a constable. I memorized the number on his shoulder, then became aware that it would not be of any help if he were not genuine.

The car park had only a handful of cars at this early hour. The constable headed for a large black Vauxhall. The windows were not exactly blacked out but I had a twinge of apprehension when I could not see inside. Then a door opened and a face appeared. "In here," said a female voice. Then, "Thank you, Constable."

The face was that of Sergeant Winifred Fletcher of Scotland Yard. It was a well-known face to me, for we had worked together on the Circle of Carême case in London. "Winsome Winnie," I had dubbed her then. "Come on in," she invited, and I climbed into the cavernous interior of the police Vauxhall. It was not really cavernous but a half-stretched model that permitted the installation of additional seats facing backwards, toward the occupants of the back seats. There was one other occupant. He was Inspector Ronald Hemingway, Winnie's superior and the head of Scotland Yard's Food Squad.

I had always thought of Hemingway as perfect Hollywood casting for the commandant of a Foreign Legion fort. His eyes seemed ideal for scanning the Sahara horizon for hordes of Bedouins, and the tight mouth under the trim mustache looked as if it should be barking commands to the guards on the battlements. He even had an erect military bearing, which aided the illusion, though the flawlessly cut suit from Gieves & Hawkes of Savile Row and the Pierre Cardin tie ruined it.

His role, and that of the Food Squad, arose out of the growing importance of food and restaurants in present-day society. Food had became a powerful and wealthy business, and like any wealthy business, it had attracted crime and criminals. Scotland Yard had had an Art Squad and a Fraud Squad for some time. Recent additions to their organization had been the Computer Squad, the Business Squad, and—most recently of all—the Food Squad. Winnie gave me an encouraging smile. I interpreted it to mean that I was not in any trouble as far as her department was concerned—not at the moment anyway.

Inspector Hemingway was already speaking and his tone was friendly. "Nice to see you again. It appears that you will be working with us once more. Let's hope it turns out as well as the Circle of Carême affair."

I looked from him to Winnie and back again. "You're part of the investigation into Kenny Bryce's death?" I asked.

"No, we are not, not yet at any rate. Sergeant, do you want to fill in the details here?"

Winnie's red-lipped smile was good to see again. In the case that Hemingway had referred to, we had become very well acquainted. From a suspect, I had progressed to a Scotland Yard helper, and from there on, Winnie and I had become—what is the euphemism?—"very good friends." I had not seen her for some time as she had been in Northern Ireland on a case, but she looked as delectable as ever. I had to force myself to pay attention to her words.

"Several cases of poisoning have come to our attention. No deaths have resulted, fortunately, which is why little publicity has been attached. The symptoms were similar, which led us to believe that all of them had a common cause. We didn't get in on these cases right away because the local police authorities didn't see any reason to report them to us. Once we were onto it, we could see what looked like a pattern.

"When the report of a poisoning here at Harlington Castle showed up, we had another piece of the puzzle. As this one resulted in a death, we were authorized to look into it."

"You've talked to Inspector Devlin, I presume."

Inspector Hemingway nodded. He had the same cool, confident look that I remembered. "Yes. That's when your name came up. She said that you had, er, mentioned working with us."

"I was trying to avoid being listed among the suspects," I said.

Hemingway's mouth twisted in a slight smile. "Well, of course, I gave you a good name. I added that that did not eliminate you as a murder suspect, but I said I doubted very much if you shared any guilt."

"Thanks," I said. "Inspector Devlin is what could be called a tough cookie."

"A very responsible officer," said Hemingway with a perfectly straight face.

"She said yesterday that she was going to issue a press release today. Is it out yet? What does it say?"

"As there are the previous poisonings to take into account now, the case here takes on a new complexion. In order to avoid spreading alarm, the release is cautiously worded—"

"Does it give the cause of Kenny Bryce's death?" I asked quickly.

"No," Hemingway said. He glanced at Winnie.

"But you know."

It was Winnie who answered. "An amino acid called boro-amine."

"I don't think I've heard of that one," I said. "Is it a known pharmaceutical compound?"

"Not much is known about it. It isn't used as a pharmaceutical compound. It has been isolated in the laboratory but no use has ever been proposed for it."

Hemingway added, "The poisoning case that we already had on our books—the one that resulted in a death—was the only one we could backtrack to, as it was the only one where we had knowledge of stomach contents. An autopsy had to be performed, and when we asked for further analysis, we had confirmation. Death was due to boro-amine."

"How could anybody get hold of it?" I wondered.

Winnie shook her head. "We don't know."

"We've asked our people in Chelmsford to synthesize some so it can be studied," Hemingway said. "We'll know more then." I knew that the Forensic Laboratory in Chelmsford had a fine reputation throughout Europe.

"Could it be related to histamine in any way?" I asked.

"Why do you ask?" Hemingway countered smoothly.

"I saw Kenny Bryce immediately after the joust. He had facial flushes, heavy perspiration, deep and irregular breathing, faint pulse—all of the classic symptoms of histamine poisoning."

Hemingway nodded. "That accounts for your unwise and premature statement to the Entertainments Director, McCartney, about him—let me see, what were your words?—ah, yes, having 'all the symptoms of having been poisoned.' "

The Food Squad had done its homework. I should not have expected anything less from them. I glanced at Winnie. There was a hint of a supportive smile there and I took encouragement from it.

"Those were my words, yes. I probably wouldn't have said them if I'd known there was an epidemic of such cases, and besides, it was disturbing to see him that way. I spoke without thinking."

"Quite understandable," Hemingway said imperturbably.

"Of course, there are other poisons that generate the same symptoms as the histamine group," I reminded him.

"Several," he agreed. "There's one other bit of information we've learned from the lab before they get their full investigation underway." He paused, then said: "Boro-amine contains a significant amount of vitamin K."

I thought about that for a moment. "Does that mean something?"

They both looked pensive, but neither spoke until Hemingway said, "Not as much as we want it to. At least, not yet." He looked at his watch. "We have to be going. Before we do, though, I wanted you to know that our investigation of those other cases was already underway. We didn't really know in which direction it was going, but this death could be the clue and may provide more data. There's one other detail . . ." He gave me his most penetrating stare.

"When we heard about this case, we had just had some computer correlation. It showed that all of the people we knew to have been affected had visited Harlington Castle recently. It took some time for this to emerge because we had to interrogate all the friends and relatives of the victims. They are not all from this area, of course.

"As a result of this, we had decided to send someone here to do some on-the-spot investigating. We are a bit shorthanded at the moment, so learning you were here was good news."

I had the sinking feeling that I had been volunteered without my cognizance.

"You mean—"

"Yes," said Inspector Hemingway. "A bit of luck for us. We have a man on the inside. You!" He tapped on the glass partition to alert the driver. "Keep us informed, won't you? Sergeant Fletcher will be your contact as before. Leave liaison with Inspector Devlin to me. And remember, no more rash diagnoses."

Winnie pulled the door open for me and I stepped out. There didn't seem much to say so I didn't say it.

It was a pleasant day with just a hint of rain in the air but also the likelihood that it might pass. As I approached the main castle building, I recognized the figure coming toward me, Don Mc-Cartney.

"Have a good day in London?" he asked. News evidently traveled fast.

I gave him a brief outline of my visits regarding both meat and fish without elaborating too much on the Seven Seas. "Sounds like you're making progress," he said.

"One thing I wanted to ask you."

"Yes, what is it?"

"I understand all supplies are purchased by a central operation. Who runs that?"

"Donna Rowlands." Then he asked, "Is there some problem with food supplies?"

I have learned that an answer to a different question often suffices when you don't want to answer the original question. "We are going to be trying some foods that haven't been served before. Hopefully, we can use the same suppliers."

He nodded. "Donna will be very helpful. She's had a lot of experience."

He left me to hurry across to the adjoining buildings. As I approached the castle doors, another figure materialized beside me. She was attractive and smartly dressed and gave me a slight smile as I opened the door for her. She went in, crossed the hall, and disappeared.

I mulled over the Seven Seas situation. I could not believe that anyone visiting the facility would be satisfied with it. Gontier's responses were not entirely satisfying. He had not visited Seven Seas for at least a year. He said that the supplies office handled the ordering and added that he "had nothing to do with that." I was just deciding that the supplies office should be my first task of the next morning when I saw a couple approaching.

Angela, the younger daughter of the Harlington clan, wore a light blue mini-slip of a dress that combined the modern with the medieval very cleverly. Her flawless complexion was without makeup, but the damp English climate kept it fresh and appealing. Her dark eyes looked bigger than ever as she introduced the young man with her. "My cousin, Neville Woodward."

He was lean, almost thin, and had an aristocratic face with a mouth that looked as if it were about to sneer. After a few minutes of conversation, I realized that I was not necessarily the target of such an expression—it was natural.

"You got out of the maze all right, I see," she said with just a tinge of amusement.

"No problem," I said, airily if untruthfully. I looked at Angela. "I'm surprised at you, though, Angela. Hope you don't send paying customers in there. You might not see them again."

Her face was all innocence. "I didn't say a word. It was Norman who directed you that way. He considers it a short cut."

"When you know it, maybe it is." I turned to Neville. "Are you active in the castle operations?"

"Good Lord, no!" He was emphatic.

"Neville's a trader, in foreign currencies."

"Are you with one of the banks in the City?" I asked.

"No. I'm an independent." He had a slightly languid air that fitted his answer. I supposed it was one of the curses of the nobility.

"He makes lots of money, don't you, Neville?"

I was not sure whether Angela was praising him or being caustic at his expense. His reply did not support either view. "Like all traders, my dear, I do, at times . . . then one experiences those other times."

"I hear the deutsche mark is on the rise," I said.

"For a while," he said dismissively. "Until the chairman of their central banking system makes his speech next month at least."

I had no idea what the deutsche mark was doing, but I wanted to see if he really was in currency or if it was just a pose. A murder on the premises makes me suspicious of almost everybody. I would have to call a knowledgeable friend and check on that answer.

We chatted about the castle and the ramifications of its myriad activities before Neville became noticeably impatient to leave. Angela darted him a swift glance, evidently recognizing the symptoms.

"We'll be off then," she said brightly. "Next time you feel like a prowl around the maze, let me know. There's a secret corner of it, called the Bower. It used to be a trysting place in the old days."

"But no longer? You mean people don't tryst any more?"

She gave me a provocative pout. "I'll take you there soon. We can find out."

Before they were out of sight, Neville's arm was around her and they were kissing. Maybe it was for my benefit or maybe cousins were closer in the country. I wondered if I had a knowledgeable friend who could answer that one, too.

CHAPTER ELEVEN

Leave liaison with Inspector Devlin to me" had been Hemingway's parting words. I knew him well enough to know that meant I did not have to tell Devlin that I was reporting to Hemingway. It was not that Hemingway was a devious man—well, that's not true, he could be extremely devious—but it was not a matter of keeping Devlin in the dark so that the Food Squad could grab the glory. The specialized involvement of the Food Squad meant that any information I unearthed could be better interpreted by them rather than the local police. "A little rationalization does wonders to clear the mind" was a suitable dictum, I reminded myself.

My intended visit to the supplies office had slipped in priority since I had been conscripted by the Food Squad. I still needed to talk to Donna Rowlands, but a morning spent in getting better acquainted with the castle and its occupants was surely more immediately useful.

The grounds were festooned with banners and flags proclaiming today as being a "Children's Festival," and figures in brilliantly colored costumes were already flitting all over the lawns, which still glistened with the remains of a morning dew. I saw Don McCartney in his role as Entertainments Director giving instructions to a group of minstrels, radiant in bright yellows, greens, and reds. Over by the tents, several horses broke into a canter, urged by leather-clad riders, apparently practicing some maneuver. The *thump-thump* of their hooves on the grass and an occasional snorted cloud of steam lent an authentic air to the proceedings.

McCartney finished speaking to the minstrels and came in my direction. "Morning," he said. "You'll enjoy today. Oh, I know it's mainly for the kids, but it's always a great day's entertainment. Adults love it as much as the kids. You're going to be around, aren't you?"

"Absolutely," I said. "Looking forward to it."

"We don't have any violent stuff, as some of the kids are quite young. A few sword fights, some wrestling with the bears, minstrel shows with some slapstick and a few pratfalls—that kind of thing. A couple of Punch-and-Judy shows, they're always popular. Don't miss the archery display, by the way. On the stage over there, we're putting on reenactments of fairy tales, and the local Shakespeare Society is doing excerpts from plays—"

"*Midsummer Night's Dream*, no doubt."

He grinned. "Naturally. They take a lot of liberties with it. Bottom dons his ass's head several times more than the script calls for, so if you're a purist . . ."

"Not on Children's Day," I told him.

He went to assist two young women in flowing robes who were having a problem locating the place where they were due to perform. Before they had gone, a man dressed as a woodsman and carrying a plastic ax came to protest that Red Riding Hood had failed to appear. "But she doesn't have any lines, does she?" asked McCartney. The woodsman admitted that she did not, whereupon McCartney rapped, "Then get any girl!"

Children were now flowing in, bringing their parents, who looked just as eager. A group of musicians was circulating. One had an instrument like a viola, another a harp, a third a flute, and a fourth tambourines. They mixed in some tunes that sounded medieval with a few Beatles numbers.

A crowd was gathering and I went over to join it. Felicity, the elder of the two Harlington girls, was the first familiar face I saw. "You're just in time," she said, helping me to squeeze through to a clear space with a good view. "I love this show. We put it on all the time, of course, but this is a special version of it for children." She pointed. "That's Daniel—and here come his Dancing Bears."

Daniel was a youngish man with a thick bush of curly hair. He had appropriately classic features and wore an outfit in light gray with scarlet piping, collar and cuffs. On his head was a peaked hat with a scarlet plume. He played a small flute with a limited range, but the bears apparently understood it. They reared on their hind legs, making the children press back with small cries of excitement. The bears twirled, dropped on all fours, and repeated their performance.

"Aren't they great!" said Felicity, clapping her hands in delight. She wore a dress in a salmon color that made her look like a slightly older version of the children around her. "I love this show."

I decided not to recount the conversation with Victor Gontier and Madeleine Bristow when I had suggested bear meat as a suitable food for the banquets. Watching the gyrating animals, I knew that the whole idea of serving bear was doomed to oblivion. They were small enough not to be menacing. They were brown and fuzzy and the children were loving them.

Felicity waved to someone on our left and a man in his late twenties came through to us. "Have you met?" Felicity asked. She introduced me and said, "This is Frank Morgan, he worked with Kenny."

He was dark and athletic-looking. He nodded.

"You're the stuntman who plays Sir Harry," I said. "Nice to meet you."

"He's on tonight, aren't you, Frank?" asked Felicity.

"Yes. Having to double up now there's only the two of us."

His complaint brought a disapproving look from Felicity, but instead of reprimanding him, she said lightly, "We're looking for a replacement. Don McCartney has an old friend coming in to talk about the job."

"Sooner the better," the stuntman said. "Can't rely on that irresponsible brother of yours. He's likely to go streaking off into the village to see that girlfriend of his and leave us all in the lurch any time."

"At least Richard is more concerned about poor Kenny's death than you are," Felicity retorted.

"He should be," said Morgan. "Kenny's death is his fault."

Felicity was about to come back with a biting response, but she glanced at me and her upbringing as a polite young woman prevailed. "This isn't the time for an argument of this nature," she said. "We'll see you later."

She took my hand and pulled me away. Frank Morgan gave me another nod and pushed his way through the crowd in the opposite direction.

"I'm sorry," she said, when we stopped after a few paces. "Richard is a little reckless, I know, and he seems to have lost his head over that girl." She stopped as she realized the unfortunate allusion, but she went on, "He really is a feeling person and he is still devastated over Kenny's death."

"I haven't seen him around at all."

"No, he's been staying out of sight. He'll be here today, though."

A troupe of stilt walkers came waddling toward us, Pied Pipers with a stream of admiring children behind them. More wandering minstrels appeared, their flute notes shrill and their drums persistent. Felicity was silent and I sensed she was depressed. "Cheer up. Try and get into the spirit of the day. It might help."

She gave me a grateful if wan smile and we turned to find people moving toward a Punch-and-Judy show that had just begun. I steered Felicity in that direction and we watched for a few minutes. "We criticize television," I said as the policeman beat Punch over the head with his truncheon, "but perhaps its violence had some origins here."

"At least this is quieter," Felicity said. "No explosions, no gunfire, and no burning buildings collapsing."

Judy was comforting Punch now that the policeman had left. "I think Punch is faking," I said.

"No, no, he's hurt. Just because he isn't bleeding—"

"He's enjoying all the attention he's getting. I'm sure I saw him wink at the audience."

"Is that your technique?" Felicity asked. "Pretending to be hurt?"

"As a technique, it has its place. It works very well."

It was good to hear her laugh, even if it was only a small chuckle. "I'll remember that—Oh, listen—" The public announcement system was telling us that the archery contest was to commence in about five minutes.

"I want to see that," Felicity said. "Richard is in it."

We passed two jugglers throwing clubs to one another and they made mock-threatening motions of throwing a couple at us. "Stop that, Carlo!" Felicity called out to an Italian-looking fellow in blue and yellow pantaloons and blouse. He grinned and threw a club straight up into the air. Another club flew at him from his partner. He deftly caught and returned it with one hand, then with the other scooped up the falling club almost as it was about to land on the grass.

"I think we'd better take refuge here," laughed Felicity. We were passing a wooden hut with a sign outside proclaiming: "Madame Kravatsky—Fortunes Told." Colored drawings of the heavens adorned the hut. "The children at the local school did all of these," Felicity said. "One of their many contributions to this fair."

We stopped to admire the drawings, nearly all of which were remarkably imaginative. One in particular had a moon with human features. I took Felicity's arm. "Look at this one," I said, and I was pointing when—

A whistling sound seemed to come out of nowhere. It turned instantly into a whirring like an overstretched spring, then, as if by magic, an arrow slammed into the wall of the hut. The head disappeared, buried deep, and the shaft still vibrated.

Felicity gasped in fear as she stared at me, eyes wide. The arrow had passed between us, missing us by inches.

CHAPTER TWELVE

Everything else forgotten for the moment, Felicity flew toward the archery range. I followed. Bales of hay had been stacked in a rough semicircle behind the targets to absorb stray arrows. A hundred paces away, a large tent had one side open. Displays around the inside held different kinds of bows and arrows and showed the assembly from individual components. Reproductions of old woodcuts and drawings depicted archers of various nations locked in battle through the centuries.

The local Archery Society had posted a large sign which stated that they were responsible for this exhibit and demonstration, but when Felicity arrived they must have wished they had kept a lower profile. Staying just barely short of profanity, Felicity gave her razor-edged opinion of their safety and security arrangements. Her eyes blazed, her hands were in constant motion, and her voice lashed them like a bullwhip. All activities ceased and everybody listened.

When a tiny fissure opened up in her tirade and one member of the society was able to get a word in, several of them went pounding across the grass to look at the offending arrow. They returned, full of chagrin and apologies, and an impromptu inquiry was immediately opened.

It was quickly evident that nothing was going to come of it. Several of them had been standing around, archers in the contest and members of the society, as well as numerous interested visitors. Some had gone outside the tent to test the pull of this or that bow, and although the society members were reluctant to admit it, it was quite possible that someone could have taken an arrow and shot it. With all the coming and going in and out, no one was sure of anything.

"Who is or has been here, I wonder?" I murmured to Felicity, half musing, but knowing that she would pick up on it. The list included Frank Morgan, the stuntman we had left a while ago; Norman and Richard, who were both accomplished archers; and Don McCartney, who occasionally participated in contests. Norman was still here, but Richard had gone, no one was sure when. Everyone present denied loosing off an arrow or seeing anyone with one in their bow.

"What's the range to the fortune-telling booth?" I asked the vice president of the Archery Society, a nervous, twittery man with bony features, doubly agitated now.

He peered beyond the tent flap. "About a hundred paces."

I looked at the targets lined up in front of the bale of hay backwall. "About the same as to the targets."

"Well, yes," he agreed. He twisted his fingers together. "I can't understand it, though. It couldn't have been anybody here, none of them would—"

"A mischievous child?" I suggested.

"Yes!" He seized on that eagerly. "It must have been."

"There are a few of them here," I noted.

"Quite a lot."

"They all seem to be with adults, though," I said. Another thought struck me. "What is the pull on these bows?"

"Forty, forty-five pounds—why do you ask? Ah, I see, yes." His face clouded. "He'd have to be a strong boy, wouldn't he?"

Felicity rejoined me. Norman was with her. "Funny business, this," he said. He was regarding me suspiciously, I thought. "An accident, don't you agree?" he asked.

"I'm not sure you really think that," I said.

Norman hesitated, rubbed his cheek, then half-smiled. "As a matter of fact, I don't. The problem is—if it wasn't an accident, what was it?"

"Kenny's death throws doubt on any incident like this." I hoped the noncommittal comment would draw him out. Was there something he wanted to tell me? I had the feeling there was, but what was holding him back? His glance flickered to Felicity but only for a split second. Why was he afraid to speak in front of her?

"I was just talking to the vice president over there," I said. "Forty pounds pull or more on those bows means it couldn't have been a child."

Norman nodded. He seemed glad to be able to be decisive on some point. "No question about that, I'd say."

"You didn't see anybody yourself? Hanging around the tent entrance? Waiting for an opportunity to step outside and let off a shot?"

He shook his head firmly. "No. I was talking to Richard about the wind. He thought we ought to delay the start till it dropped. It can spoil an event like this."

"Did it drop?" Felicity asked.

"Well, yes, it did." His eyes searched her face.

"That's really important, isn't it?" She was trying to get out of him what he knew or what he thought, just as I was.

"I see what you're saying," he said slowly. "If the arrow was aimed at either one of you, just a breeze could have caused a miss."

"Which brings us to the other question." She turned to me. "Which of us was the target?"

"I can't believe anyone wants to stop the menu being changed," I said lightly. I wanted to retract the words as soon as they were out of my mouth but life doesn't provide reruns. I saw her mouth quiver, and added quickly, "But then nobody could want to kill you either. No, it must have been a silly accident."

I saw another familiar face coming out of the crowd around the tent. It was Neville Woodward, whom Angela had introduced as her cousin. "You both okay?" he asked, but he didn't appear too solicitous. We assured him we were, but before we could say anything more, Lord Harlington came striding across the lawn.

"I just heard. What is this all about?"

Heads turned and conversation quieted as everyone wanted to hear what the lord of the manor had to say. He noticed the change his arrival had brought about and waved to the people around the tent. "It's all right, no harm done," he called out. "Don't want this to spoil the festival."

He took us aside and asked for a detailed account. Felicity gave him one, keeping it brief but not sparing the criticism. "I just stopped by the fortune-telling booth on the way here, saw the arrow," Lord Harlington said, appalled. "My God, it could have killed you!"

"Well, it didn't, Daddy, so stop worrying. Just an accident." Felicity had recovered her composure and was making light of the incident. We talked for a few more minutes, Felicity steering the conversation further and further away from archery.

Her father left us, counseling us to be careful. Norman went with him. "I'm going to watch the dance troupe," Neville said. "They're doing sarabandes and gavottes and some of those other real old dances. Want to come along?" He ignored me, directing his question at Felicity.

"Go ahead," I told her. "Have a good time."

She smiled and the two of them walked away. I watched an acrobatic team that strolled across the grass, tossing their smaller members into the air and catching them expertly. I might have spent more time here at the Children's Festival, but I decided it was too dangerous a place for me. I walked off toward the castle where the supplies office sounded safer.

The business wing of the castle was just like the interior of any large and busy company. Some rooms had been converted into offices, the larger ones partitioned to provide working cubicles.

Phones rang, computer screens glowed, keyboards rattled, and men and women bustled around, some with papers in their hands, others with cups of tea.

"Supplies" was a fair-sized operation, handling such diverse commodities as toilet paper, feed for the horses, wax for the wooden floors, stationery and candles for the chapel. Donna Rowlands was telling me this after accepting my visit without question. She was a plump girl with horn-rimmed glasses and a crowded but not untidy desk.

"But it's the food you're interested in talking about," she concluded.

"Right," I agreed, coming straight to the point. "I would have wanted to talk to you anyway, but I was at Seven Seas and that's what I'd like to discuss first."

"The seafood people. What do you want to know?"

"Quality-control visits. Who visits them and how often?"

She reached for a file. I saw that the big label said "QC." She turned the pages.

"Victor does that," she said. "On an annual basis."

I didn't respond immediately and she was quick to frown. "Something wrong?"

"Routine, I take it?"

"Yes."

"Do you have copies of his reports?"

"No, they're kept in the office at the kitchens." She wasn't satisfied with my diversion. "Nothing wrong, is there?" she asked.

"Just details," I said airily, and she looked relieved.

"How about bread?" I asked before she could pursue her question.

"We buy from a bakery in Stony Stratton."

"That's near here, isn't it?"

"About fifteen minutes in a bakery van. That's one reason we chose it. Always fresh. 'The Muffin Man.' "

"Is that what it's called? Cute name."

"They have a good product and they're reliable. Do you want to go and see them?"

"Yes. I'd like to talk to them about the possibility of rye and barley breads. The wheat bread you serve now is not bad, but one of these others should be more tasty and also more authentic."

She reached for the phone. "I'll tell them you're coming."

"I'd rather you didn't. Bakeries run all the time anyway."

She released the instrument reluctantly. "They often like some warning—"

"This isn't a QC visit. Just a few questions. Who's your contact there?"

She opened her book again. "That's funny. We don't have a name—I wonder why?"

I wondered too. The operation at Harlington Castle seemed generally sound but there were some gaps. I went down a different avenue.

"Vegetables—there's an aspect we haven't touched on yet," I said.

Donna pushed her glasses back on her nose and smiled. "We grow most of those ourselves. You've heard about Miss Felicity's Plantation, I'm sure?"

"I have heard about it and I've been wanting to see it. I must do that right away."

"Oh, you must. She's so proud of it. Yes, she grows most of our vegetables and some of our fruit, too. Some of the exotic ones we have to buy in, like pineapples and oranges and grapefruit, but she grows kiwis, strawberries, and figs in her greenhouses."

"A clever girl," I commented.

The phone rang and I left her to wrangle over changes in delivery dates.

CHAPTER THIRTEEN

The Muffin Man was in a smart, neat-looking building on the outskirts of Stony Stratton. The village itself was pretty, well kept, with flowers everywhere. It was the next morning. Clouds scudded low and tried to look threatening but it was mostly bluff. Behind the clouds, blue sky showed and a coy sun peeked through more and more, like a bashful child increasingly bold in showing its face.

The reception area of The Muffin Man was tiny. They evidently did not do much receiving. A young girl with a ponytail slid open a plastic panel. "Was there something?"

I explained that I was at the castle and working with the chefs. I said I wanted to see the bakery facilities and discuss their products. She looked nonplussed, as if no one had ever asked this before. "We don't get visitors."

I gave her my best smile. Sometimes it works. "I'm not a visitor. I just want to look around. The castle is one of your biggest customers."

She shook her head. "You have to see the Muffin Man."

"I thought this was The Muffin Man."

"It's the name of the bakery, right. But it's the Muffin Man that owns it. Like the owner."

"Fine. I'll see him," I told her.

"Can't, he's not here."

"When is he here?"

For some reason, that question baffled her. She looked at a

blank sheet of paper that was on the desk but found no inspiration. She turned to look behind her but there was nobody there.

"I really need to see someone," I said, pleasantly, but putting a steely ring into the words. The girl was young enough to be intimidated, I reasoned. Maybe she was, but she was also persistent.

"We don't really have anybody—"

"Every business has somebody," I assured her. "The master baker will do. If he's busy, his assistant. If he's busy—"

"Just a minute." She went to a desk just far enough away that I could not hear her words on the phone as she talked with her back to me. She came back. "Just a minute," she said again.

I waited. There were no chairs, so I stood. I fidgeted and drummed fingers. I walked to and fro; the space was almost big enough for three paces each way. The girl left the panel open but ignored the manifestations of my impatience. Finally, a door opened and a young woman came in, wiping her hands on her apron, which had small hunks of dough stuck here and there.

"May," she said.

At first, I thought she was telling me when to come back, but after I told her who I was and why I was here, I found out that her name was May. I went through my presentation about the castle once more. "So I'd like to see the bakery," I said, "and talk to someone about some different breads, say rye and barley for a start."

She looked nervous. She was petite, with a sweet face and light blond hair that was in a net, presumably to keep it out of machinery. She put up a good defense but I was determined and dogged. She caved in reluctantly. "I can't spare long," she said, and I jumped in with, "Neither can I, but I appreciate your co-operation."

My desire to learn about the workings of The Muffin Man had been inspired, strangely enough, by the mystery of the *Mary Celeste*. One of the most famous ships ever to put to sea, the *Mary*

Celeste was found drifting in the Atlantic in the 1870s with not a soul on board. The vessel was in good condition, with ample supplies of food and fresh water. Speculation as to the fate of the crew has continued for more than a hundred years with scores of guesses as to the nature of the danger on board that caused the crew to abandon ship and not one of them ever to be heard of again.

It has become the most renowned of all naval mysteries and new theories continue to emerge. One recent theory has gained considerable support, and in my line of work, it had a particular fascination. I was determined to establish if it could be considered as a possible explanation for the poisonings at Harlington Castle.

Ergot, a fungus, infects cereal grains and especially rye. Rye thrived in the cool, damp climates of Northern Europe—the same climates that killed wheat, so rye was widely used for breadmaking. Unfortunately, those same climatic conditions make rye susceptible to ergot. It is believed that many deaths among crew members of sailing ships were due to ergotic poisoning: the fungus spreads rapidly through the rye flour carried on such ships. On transatlantic voyages, cold and damp were prevalent, and long periods at sea enabled the fungus to do its deadly work quite unsuspected. This was the reasoning that pointed a finger at rye in the *Mary Celeste* case.

Historians have long known that many communities too suffered horrifying disasters as a result of this insidious poison. After centuries of peaceful living, the Scandinavians suddenly and destructively erupted into the violence of the Viking period, burning churches and monasteries, razing crops and carrying off women. In the Rhine Valley in the ninth century, over ten thousand people died, poisoned by ergotic rye bread. In the seventeenth century, extraordinary outbursts from "witches" among the young girls of Salem in Massachusetts resulted in twenty of them being put to death. They claimed to have sensations of flying, to have experienced visions and heard voices. Children in local villages died in unprecedented numbers and cattle deaths were at a previously unknown level.

In all of these cases, rye bread was the staple diet. It is impossible to prevent ergot from contaminating the rye flour and ergot contains two dozen poisons. One of these is the hallucinogen LSD, which certainly could account for the exceptional behavior of the girls in Salem. Some unaccountable bloodstains on the deck of the *Mary Celeste* could have been due to a few crew members running amok with axes or knives. Perhaps the survivors jumped overboard in their madness.

I thought back to the symptoms of Kenny Bryce as he lay on the cot after the joust: severe abdominal pains, temporary blindness, delirium, and convulsions—the same symptoms that are associated with ergot poisoning. But other poisons can cause these symptoms, so maybe I was going down a cul-de-sac. But I felt I had to follow this possibility.

We toured the plant. Mills ground down the flour, which went into stainless-steel vats to ripen, aging until it was just right for breadmaking. The air was thick with the rich, strong smell. It went into the mixers, where water, yeast, vitamins, and minerals were added, forming a sponge. After further mixing, this went into the fermentation room. Here, the sponge rose and was returned to the mixer, where salt, sugar, milk powder, water, and other ingredients depending on the type of bread were added. Further fermentation followed, then the dough was shaped; the carbon dioxide from fermenting was forced out; and finally came the baking operation.

It was fascinating, especially watching the brown, slightly steaming loaves come marching triumphantly out of the ovens in trim, soldierlike lines. But I was itching to get to the storage rooms. If ergot was being allowed to grow, this was where it would be.

There was no suggestion of it. Storage was under humidity-controlled conditions and no possibility of ergotine poisoning existed. Determined to be really thorough, I browsed around until I located the rye flour. It was the right color—no trace of the pinkish tinge that would warn of incipient ergotism.

I could see nothing at all to cause quality problems—and that thought led to my asking, "How long is it since you were visited by someone from the castle?" But May looked vague and said she was not sure.

We concluded the tour in the shipping and packaging area. May did not plan on showing me these, saying they were not very interesting, but I insisted. She was right, they were not interesting, but both areas were impeccable. May gave me a look which said she hoped I was leaving. "Just one more thing," I said, and repeated my intention to furnish visitors to the castle with rye bread and barley bread.

She blinked at me. "We do make pumpernickel—it's made from coarse rye, you know—but it's not a real big seller in the local shops."

"Pumpernickel does have a limited market," I agreed, "but made as a medieval bread, maybe not quite as heavy and served as part of a medieval meal, it might go down well. We could take quite a lot of it."

"All right. Now, barley is difficult to hull. That makes the bread more expensive. Still," she said, looking like a pensive schoolgirl pondering an awkward part of the eleven times table, "rye and barley both mix well with wheat, and that restores the fiber level as well as keeping the calorie count down."

It was my turn to blink. May knew about bread for sure. "Could you bake a few dozen loaves of each of those?" I asked. "We'll give them a try. See how the customers react."

She stood there with a dubious look on her face.

"What's wrong?" I asked. "You have to check with the Muffin Man?"

"Er, yes," she murmured finally. Perhaps she was merely pursuing the baking angle in her mind because, after a pause, she said, "We could use rye flour, mix in some yellow cornmeal"—she stopped to think some more, then went on—"add some dark unsulfured molasses and some buttermilk."

"Sounds great. Let's try that."

We went on past the baking ovens and the smell was almost irresistible. She didn't exactly show me out. She took me to the door, gave me a demure nod, and disappeared back inside.

The song from childhood came to my mind, drifting up from schooldays. "Do you know the Muffin Man?" I didn't know him any better now than I had before. The song went on to say that "he dwells in Drury Lane," but this one didn't. He didn't even dwell in Stony Stratton. He was proving more elusive than the Pimpernel.

The Children's Festival was over when the taxi dropped me at the gates of Harlington Castle. The cleanup crew had swept through like a tornado and hardly a trace remained from the invasion of the little darlings. A single, forlorn ice cream wrapper had escaped and lay desecrating the lawn. I picked it up and dropped it into the nearest barrel.

In the main hall, a constable was putting on his helmet as he hurried out. Don McCartney, the entertainments director, came through a side door and, seeing me, came over. "That inspector is a demon, isn't she?"

"Very formidable," I said cautiously. "Has she been grilling you?"

"She's been asking a lot of questions," he protested.

"She seems to be good at that."

"Anyway, how are you getting along? Making progress?"

I gave him the briefest of summaries of my visits to the Smithfield Market, the fish supplier, and The Muffin Man. I gave him the facts only, no comments.

"Speaking of meat," he said, "I suppose you'll be at the culling of the deer herds tomorrow?"

"Haven't heard about it. Victor Gontier did mention that they were culled occasionally and that was when venison went on the menu. I didn't know it was tomorrow, though."

"Yes, it is. All our crack shots will be there."

"Not with bows and arrows, I hope?"

"Bows and—? Oh, I see. Yes, I heard about that incident. Some careless idiot."

"Probably," I agreed.

"No, bows and arrows aren't allowed for this kind of thing. The Forestry Commission has strict laws about how herds are culled. Only high-powered rifles."

"Crack shots, you said. Who are your crack shots?" I asked casually.

"Lord Harlington has declined this year."

"Does he usually participate?"

"This will be the first year he hasn't, but Richard and Norman will be there, of course, and their cousin, Neville. I will be there, and three of our riders who are expert shots. Miss Angela insists on taking part, too," he added in a sort of neutral voice.

"She's a bit of a tomboy, isn't she?"

"She certainly is." His voice hid some of his disapproval. Some came through, though I wasn't sure whether it was for Angela or for women in general who participated in such masculine activities.

"Can she qualify as a crack shot?"

"She certainly can. With rifle and pistol both."

"How about with a bow and arrow?" I put the question half-jokingly.

McCartney took it the same way. With a slight smile, he said, "I think Nature's against her there. I don't think she could pull a forty-pound bow."

We chatted a little longer, then we parted. He had to receive a delegation of travel agents from Canada, so I went to the kitchens.

A dark blue van idled outside the back door as I approached. It started up and drove off. I went in to find Madeleine Bristow, the red-cheeked young Lancashire woman who was assistant to Victor Gontier, the head chef. She looked a little flustered and was stroking her hair back into place. A clandestine visit from an admirer (as they called them in Victorian days), I thought, so I put on my most professional air to make it clear that her lovelife was none of my business.

"The Muffin Man is sending some rye loaves and some barley loaves," I told her. "Perhaps you can keep track of how they go compared to the wheat and white loaves you usually serve."

She nodded.

"I had dinner with the guests," I told her. "They all enjoyed it. The sole was popular and the veal roast was very good."

She nodded again, this time with a little enthusiasm. I guessed she was anxious to talk about food rather than her morning visitor.

"We might think again about frumenty as an accompaniment to the main meat course," I suggested. "Or blancmange, the non-sweetened version. Something different from rice or potatoes."

"We could make frumenty the way you mentioned," she said. "Leave out the almonds maybe. And what about polenta?"

The cornmeal porridge is a staple of Northern Italian cooking. "Not exactly English medieval," I said, "but it's a good idea. Dishes going with main meat courses need to show more variety. Cool the polenta after cooking, then fry it in slices is maybe the best way. It doesn't have a great deal of flavor."

"As much as potato," Madeleine argued, "and there are ways of increasing the flavor. Garlic, flecks of sun-dried tomato."

"That's true." I was glad to be getting some input. "The Corsican style is to use chestnut flour. That's much tastier."

"How about mixing that with the cornmeal? We could get some interesting combinations."

"Good. Will you try that?"

She assented eagerly. "Victor is over in the main dining room. I'll talk to him as soon as he comes back. He's anxious to try some eels, by the way."

"Good. And I hear venison is going to be on the menu," I

said. We discussed the times and ways of hanging it. Then I said, "Talking about food always makes me hungry. What's on the menu for lunch today?" She listed the courses for me and I decided to have something light with the staff. "And I've looked up one or two of my old cookbooks," she told me. "Rissoles should be popular. I'm going to try some tomorrow."

"Try them out on the staff," I suggested. "I'll have some, too." I turned to go, then remembered, "By the way, we have to do something about the desserts. They have become a bit routine."

"I was thinking about those, too. I'll have some suggestions for you by tomorrow."

She was getting almost bubbly by now. I was making some progress.

CHAPTER FOURTEEN

Frank Morgan, the other stuntman who played Sir Harry Mountmarchant, was in the staff cafeteria and gave me a nod. I saw a thick mop of curly hair and recognized Daniel, he of the Dancing Bears. Lisa, the West Indian woman from the library, was just leaving and gave me a smile. The diminutive Eddie was there too, with three or four cronies—that word seemed to suit his table companions perfectly. They were engaged in a story-swapping contest, it appeared, and gales of high-pitched laughter kept breaking out, so I left them to it.

A radicchio and endive salad seemed like a good idea for starting the meal. Unfortunately, the walnut vinaigrette was applied a bit too lavishly and too early, making the whole thing a little soggy. Fish and chips, one of the choices to follow, had a number of takers, but it was a bit too heavy for me, so I had a bowl of mussels in white wine with a slice of Italian bread. Instead of wine, I had a glass of Malvern water and left feeling quite virtuous.

I inquired after Felicity in the main dining room and was told she had already eaten a light meal and left. After making inquiries of two staff members and one policeman, I learned that she had gone to the library, so I made my way there. It had that musty and quite unmistakable smell of old paper, leather, and wood polish. The vaulted ceiling soared high, allowing shelves to climb the paneled walls to heights that could be reached only by sliding ladders. Footsteps echoed on the polished floorboards and lamps under green shades cast pools of orange light.

Books dominated the scene, obviously, most of them in leather bindings and many gilt-lettered. Scattered around were busts perched on columns, while some shelves had a royal seal or a miniature attached. The feeling of antiquity was alleviated only by the unexpectedly clean and tidy appearance of the room and I congratulated Lisa on it. "Mustn't be easy," I added.

Her milk chocolate brown face smiled to show perfect white teeth. "Well, we don't get too many customers," she said.

"I see Felicity is one of them, though." She was at the end of the room, absorbed in a large tome, and had not seen me.

"Oh, she's a regular visitor. Plants and all that kind of thing fascinate her."

"So this must be where she got all the information for her Plantation."

"Yes—and she still does."

Felicity had heard our voices. She spotted me and came to join us. She still had a book in her hands—both hands, for it was a formidable volume. She saw me trying to catch a glimpse of the title and held it up for me to see. *Forgotten Plants*, the title read.

"Sounds fascinating," I said.

"Some plants go out of fashion—like clothes and food and lots of other things. Others—never actually in fashion—just go unnoticed."

"And you bring them back from oblivion," I said.

"I like to do that whenever I can. You'd be interested in some of them—the ones you can eat."

"I certainly would," I said. "Lost leeks, overlooked onions—there's always a market for a food that's new and different, even if it's not really new but a grafted version of an old one, or a vegetable from the past just coming around again. Which reminds me—I still haven't seen your Plantation."

She put the book down on a shiny tabletop. "Like to see it?"

"Very much."

"Right now?"

"This very minute."

She patted the book affectionately. "Thanks, Lisa. I'll be back for another session with this." She took my arm as if she had known me for years. "Let's go."

It was well named "The Plantation." It was a mini-farm, cleverly laid out and well kept. Felicity delighted in showing me every plant, vegetable, and flower. A dozen varying shades of green were highlighted with splashes of color.

"I placed it away from trees, buildings, and hedges so that it is not shaded," she explained. It was far removed from the castle, I noted. "I like to get every ray of sunshine on it that I can," she added.

She referred to each plant and vegetable by name as if it were a personal friend. "Vegetables that grow well in the English climate are the primary aim," she said. I could see beans, carrots, cauliflower, broccoli, spinach, lettuce, radishes, parsnips, peas, cucumbers. "Onions and potatoes somewhere," I commented.

"Over here," she said. "We use lots of those. Oh, and over there, we grow courgettes and melons together. They are related so they can be rotated as a team."

Trellises were erected here and there. They were on the north side so as to throw no shadow. "It's early for the blackberries," Felicity said, "but these will be covered." Teepees of poles provided support for plants that needed to climb.

"Nice color balance here," I complimented her. Broccoli foliage lent a pleasing blue contrast to the green all around.

"And then this way we have our herb garden." There was chervil, dill, parsley, sage, basil, rosemary, marjoram, mint, chives, and others, all laid out in neat plots. I noticed lovage, nearly six feet high, with its small golden flowers at the top. Walkways of stone slab and brick looked like miniature roads through the countryside.

Apples, pears, and cherries had a large plot of their own. "Then there's the greenhouses for potting," Felicity said, "and also for the fruits that don't grow well outdoors."

"You've done a wonderful job here," I told her.

"We don't supply all our vegetable needs, of course, but a good share of them," she said proudly. "Even less of the fruit needs, but that's because so many of them come from warmer climes than ours. Oh, we can grow oranges and lemons, but only about a quarter of what we need. We even have bananas and pineapples, but that's only to prove they can be grown in greenhouses. We have to buy in most of the exotic fruit, naturally. I was in America last year and arranged to buy seeds for growing mangoes, guava, and papaya."

"There aren't many fruits and vegetables you don't grow," I commented.

She paused to pull a few dead stalks. "I don't grow any poisonous ones," she said.

You're a very perceptive girl," I told her, "but you weren't mind-reading. I wasn't thinking that at all. I really was admiring what you've accomplished."

She turned her classic features toward me. "The point was bound to arise eventually. If you didn't bring it up, that inspector would. She gives me the creeps, that woman. Must make her a good policewoman, I suppose."

"She is formidable," I agreed. "As to the ready availability of all the veggies that go into a salad, the country is full of gardens and allotments that do that."

"He's my brother; of course I know his likes and dislikes. Add your comments about Kenny being poisoned and, well, it all adds up, doesn't it?"

"It's not certain—"

"Not altogether, no." She wafted a few fruit flies away.

"Besides, if Kenny was poisoned, we don't know if it was by the vegetables you're growing here."

"Someone was trying to kill Richard." She said it with a dreadful air of finality.

"Do you have some reason to believe that someone would want to?"

"He was out riding two weeks ago. His horse threw him."

"That could easily be an—"

"No, it wasn't an accident. The saddle straps were frayed through."

"Carelessness in the stables?"

"The groom swears that the saddle that was supposed to be used was nearly new. Somehow, an old one was substituted. One that had only a few strands left. It was bound to break."

"At the time, I suppose you merely thought it was a mistake?"

"Exactly." She sounded relieved that I understood. "I mean, it takes a lot to make you suspect a deliberate attempt to take someone's life, doesn't it? But now, with Kenny dying like this . . ."

I stopped by a magnificent row of strawberry bushes. "And what about you? Was that arrow really an accident?" I asked.

She plucked a strawberry, bit into it, then plucked another and handed it to me. "It's all right—it's safe to eat. We don't use any harmful sprays."

It was delicious, rich and luscious. "The arrow must have been an accident," she said. "Nothing else makes any sense."

She was still savoring the taste of the strawberry, rolling it round her tongue. "Unless it was aimed at you," she added reflectively.

We strolled back to the castle, our walk punctuated by sporadic bursts of thought and speculation. "What does Richard think about all this?" I asked.

"He's an ostrich. Thinks any suggestion that someone would want to kill him is nonsense."

"What about Norman and Angela?"

"Selfish pigs, both of them."

I caught her eye and she laughed. "Well, they are. Don't think beyond themselves. If it doesn't happen to them, they don't even care about it."

We walked on in silence and were coming onto the lawn approaching the castle.

"Do you know Richard's girlfriend?" I asked suddenly.

If it caught her unawares, I didn't gain anything by it. She paused before answering, but not in a way that indicated she needed to think about her answer.

"Jean Arkwright, her name is. I've seen her in the village. Had her pointed out to me in the Post Office where she was working. Naturally, we in the family have this social gap that we're sensitive about. She isn't good enough for 'our Richard.' That's the Harlington stance."

"Understandable."

"She's a nice enough girl from all accounts."

"Is it just an infatuation or may it be the real thing?"

She sighed loudly. "Wish we knew. Father doesn't understand how it could be anything else other than infatuation, naturally. Angela dismisses it, thinks it'll pass with time, but then she tends to be a flibbertigibbet herself so she thinks it readily of others."

I smiled at the Elizabethan expression. She went on, "Norman isn't too concerned about it, one way or the other."

"And Richard? What does he say?"

"He says it's none of our business—which is wrong, it is our business if he gets serious."

"And you think he is?"

"He should be at the age where he can recognize the difference."

We were on the banks of the castle moat by now. The walls towered up to the first level of parapets, the thousand-year-old masonry impassive, seeming to offer its own comment on the family problem.

"Thanks for the tour of the Plantation," I said. "I've been looking forward to it and the reports have not been exaggerated. It really is a wonderful achievement."

"Good." She said the word like a polite young lady, then changed her image completely by standing on tiptoe and giving me a firm kiss on the lips. "Nice of you to listen to the trials and tribulations of the Harlington clan. Next time, we'll talk about more pleasant topics."

"I hope next time is soon," I called out as she walked away.

A footman came up to me as I walked across the hall. He held a slip of paper in his hand. "Excuse me, sir, this gentleman wants you to call him."

I did.

It was Edgar Sampson and he answered promptly. "Listen, I have to go to the London Heralds' Society day after tomorrow. I wondered if you might want to go with me?"

The London Heralds' Society is the core of the genealogical information network in the country. Most of their business comes from overseas, particularly Americans, Australians, Canadians, and others who want to have their ancestors traced. This is partly because they hope to hear that they are descended from royalty. At the same time, the heralds themselves, skilled at the subterfuge inherent in the spider's web of ancestral heritage, know just how to conceal the presence in the past of pickpockets, footpads, horse thieves, rogues, and vagabonds.

Still, more dexterity is required when fleshing out characters in bygone centuries who may be open to a considerable amount of interpretation. While the client might not want to admit to a robber in the family tree, a highwayman with his tricornered hat, his black mask, and his pistol might be acceptable as a romantic figure. Similarly, while harlots and strumpets would be frowned upon, courtesans and mistresses might be tolerated as racily romantic and worth a few points in a game of one-upmanship in the social contest. The heralds are expert at this—and who can say their interpretation is inaccurate after the passage of a century or three?

I knew some of this and Edgar filled me in on the rest. He continued: "You said you were interested in the Harlington family.

The fellow I'm seeing knows more scuttlebutt than anyone else there at the society. After I'm done, you can ask him a few of your questions."

"Sounds like a good idea," I said. "Let me see if I can get a day pass out of prison here."

"That lady inspector keeping you penned in, is she?" asked Edgar with a chuckle at his own wit.

We made arrangements to meet and I went for a hot bath, then a scotch and soda and dinner.

CHAPTER FIFTEEN

The kitchen did a good job with dinner that evening. A goat cheese salad with the pungency of raspberry vinegar, the added crispness of endives, and a sprinkling of raisins and pine nuts set the mood. The endives were French rather than the usual Belgian; these are curly and many find them tastier.

I followed with a Carbonnades, a variant on beef stew, in the Flemish style. This has onions, bacon slices, and boneless beef stewing meat cut into cubes. The seasonings are thyme and bayleaf only, but added flavor comes from wine vinegar and brown sugar. The stock is only partly beef broth as the rest is a full-bodied ale. Noodles are the best accompaniment and these were just al dente.

Different versions of this dish abound. In Arles, they use olives and tomatoes; in Lyon, they garnish with wild mushrooms. The Cypriot style is seasoned with cinnamon and cloves, while the Spaniards deviate furthest of all. Their stew, known as *Cocido*, has sausages, green beans, and potatoes. The one I was eating was a true Carbonnades and one of those examples of a dish which is truly at its best when kept simple. Some medieval dishes were on the menu but it could be argued that a stew with a minimum of ingredients like this one must surely be of ancient origin.

Some fresh peaches were among the choices for dessert and I checked with the waitress to make sure they were from Felicity's Plantation. They were. The chef had warmed them in Burgundy with just a drizzle of honey and they were superb.

I took a stroll afterwards by way of aiding the digestion. The night was cool but pleasant and I gazed into the moat for inspiration. Felicity's story of Richard's earlier incident with the frayed saddle was not convincing evidence of a murder attempt on its own, but coupled with the poisoning of Kenny by boro-amine it made a much stronger case.

The moat provided little inspiration.

Despite the impressive array on the buffet table the next morning, I ate a very light breakfast—orange juice, corn flakes with a banana, and coffee. I wanted to have a clear head for observing the culling of the deer herd.

I had not been invited to take an active part, which was understandable. They wanted to rely on marksmen proven accurate on earlier shoots, for a clean kill is important, not only for humanitarian reasons but so as to minimize damage to the carcass. Not that I would have accepted even if invited, for I detest firearms. I was curious to see the ritual, though.

We gathered at the main entrance. The shooters all wore appropriate dress—light tweeds. Ten or so others were there, including Felicity and Angela.

"I'm disappointed," I told them. "I thought I'd see at least one female gun."

Angela wrinkled her nose. "Daddy is a Neanderthal when it comes to activities like this. If there were ever a secret ballot on the subject, I'll bet he'd be against women voting and driving cars."

All three shooters wore slacks and jackets, not quite sporty but outdoorsy. "At least, you don't pursue them on horseback, like a foxhunt," I commented.

Felicity shook her head. "It isn't a hunt. All they're doing is culling the herd."

The roar of engines reverberated across the lawn. Four Land Rovers, modified with extra seats, were followed by a one-and-a-half-ton pickup truck. They pulled up near us and we climbed in the Land Rovers. The drive took us out into the estate grounds west of the castle, a parklike area, thick with gorse and frequent stands of oak and beech. We stopped; the drivers conferred, shouting over the engine noise; then we went on across the seemingly boundless acres of the Harlington estate.

The sky was clear but for some fleeting high nimbus. It was an ideal day. After more bumping over the grass, we stopped to park the vehicles by some massive oaks. The park led off to the near horizon in waves of soft green.

"Over there," said Norman.

The shooters had alighted and were in a tight bunch, rifles on one shoulder and bandoliers over the other. Norman pointed to a cluster of gorse that had grown to a height of ten feet and covered an area half the size of a football field. At first, none of us could see any movement. Then some sharp eye called out, "On the left—look!"

The head of a deer poked out of a bush, looking around speculatively. "Has it smelled us?" I asked. Richard shook his head. He seemed to be in command of the unit. "They might have heard the engines." He motioned to the others and they fanned out, moving forward.

"Are they trying to flush the deer out of those bushes?" I asked.

"Yes," said Angela, who appeared to be well informed, perhaps from previous culls. "They don't want to stampede them, though. Shooting them when they're on the run is hunting technique but they might not get a clean kill that way. In a cull, you want to be sure to kill, not just maim."

Her eyes were bright, almost predatory, and she was clearly enjoying this. "Let's go this way, the view will be better," she said, "as the ground gets higher."

Felicity was watching the shooters, now disappearing over a rise. "I think I'll follow the men with the guns," she said.

"Do as you please," said Angela with a shrug. She turned to me. "Coming?" Her eyes were inviting.

We walked over the thick grass; the slope was gently but firmly rising. We could see further now and could make out two of the shooters, some distance apart. Felicity was closing up to them. The others had moved out of sight.

"I suppose they have to make sure they don't hit each other," I commented.

"Oh, they've all done this before," Angela said. "Each has his own field of fire."

The slope was getting steeper and the going slower. We could see three figures now, quite distinctly. One of them was Felicity, but then they all moved out of sight.

We went on up the slope, finally approaching a copse of trees where work had evidently been done recently: cut lengths of tree trunk were neatly stacked.

"A good place for a breather," Angela said. I needed it, for the climb had been steady. She led the way to some stumps that had been sawn at a height making them ideal stools. We had just reached them when—

The crack of the rifle merged into a hollow whine. A bullet smacked into a tree near us and I stood for a second, rooted to the spot. I looked around for some better shelter. The big oaks were of limited use, for if the person with the gun moved to change the angle, we would be exposed. A matted tangle of high bushes caught my eye. I grabbed Angela's hand and dragged her in that direction. I was expecting to hear a further crack of gunfire at any second. We dived into the bushes, less concerned about thorns than bullets, but we encountered neither. I realized that these were ferns, soft and comforting. We scrambled deeper, pushing the ferns aside, then collapsed onto a flattened area.

As we rolled over closely entwined, Angela squeezed against me, breath coming in gulps, the danger of being shot declining in importance. Her large dark eyes searched my face. She squeezed closer. We kissed, then again more passionately.

Then several times more . . . I was floating in a sensuous world of soft flesh and a faint but indeterminable perfume. Perhaps it was not perfume at all but a natural and delightful personal fragrance. I was swallowed up in that world and sank deeper and deeper into it. Hazy, exciting mental images swam through my brain and I lost track of time as I floated through space . . .

My vision cleared. I found myself gazing into a pair of eyes. They were large and brown and beautiful. I was prepared to lose myself in them again when I felt a vague stirring of something wrong . . .

I tried to push the notion aside but it would not go away. Something was amiss. I struggled to think what it could be, then the thought crystallized. Those eyes!

What had happened to Angela's eyes? They were darker but not as large. They were even a different shape.

The eyes examined me with mild curiosity. A pink tongue appeared, the tip moving slowly and provocatively. It was when a small nose, twitching very slightly, appeared below it among the ferns that I came out of my romantic haze.

The face that was inches away belonged to a fawn, a baby deer. It must have been very young and its parents had not yet taught it to beware of those dangerous beings—humans. The shapely head half-turned as another appeared beside it. This one must have been a few months older, for it was larger and looked more suspicious. Another head poked through and studied us. We might have been models for a class of student deer.

I shook Angela. She gasped some words. I didn't catch any of them except for "again," then she became aware that I was being distracted. She was starting to get critical about my attention span when she realized that parts of our surroundings were displaying movement. Her eyes widened. The ferns had parted to admit one more curious face and then another.

Angela struggled to her feet, making scathing and unladylike criticisms of the dainty creatures around us. It dawned on me that these ferns were their favorite eating and the parents had probably deposited their offspring here as a sort of Nature's day nursery—one with a built-in food supply.

Slowly and carefully, I parted the ferns to see a clearing where a dozen of the tiny, graceful creatures were nibbling away. Food was of more interest to them than two members of a strange subspecies engaged in some bizarre ritual.

I hated to disturb their tea party but neither could I make it clear to them that this was a matter of life and death. It was probably just as well, because it would be too complicated to disassociate ourselves from those other humans out there with guns. Given some means of communication, I could at least have clarified that those men shooting at their parents were shooting at me too.

Deer, I was beginning to appreciate, were not unlike other species of animal life. They varied from one to another; they had different reactions. A couple of them were flicking their tails in an edgy, twitchy sort of way, unhappy at this invasion of their haven. One of them looked downright aggressive, though disqualified, by its size, weight, and lack of horns, from doing anything about it. A couple looked genuinely curious and slightly puzzled. The others just couldn't care less as long the stock of ferns held up.

Angela was fastening buttons, pulling zippers and brushing off her clothes, giving small sighs of exasperation. She blew out her cheeks in one final gasp, then became very matter-of-fact.

"I think the shooting party has moved away," she said.

"What makes you think that?"

"I haven't heard any gunfire for some time."

I thought there might be another reason why she had not heard anything for some time, but decided not to infringe on her irritated mood.

We made our cautious way back to the edge of the thicket. There was nothing and no one in sight. The crack of a rifle sounded and it was a long way away. "It's safe," said Angela authoritatively. "Come on."

CHAPTER SIXTEEN

Culling a deer herd was no longer as interesting as it had been. We were first to return to the vehicles and we stood by one of the Land Rovers.

"It was only one shot," Angela said. She had been making the point that it could have been an accidental discharge of a weapon or a shooter becoming disoriented and not realizing that we were in his line of fire.

"There was only one arrow too," I reminded her. "At Felicity and me."

"What's your point?" she asked, turning to face me. She had been argumentative and confrontational since we left the fawns' picnic ground, perhaps in frustration. A frolic in the ferns was probably her intention—or was there more to it than that? I didn't feel like debating the meaning of it, suspecting that it would be a debate I would lose.

"Either one alone could be an accident. Two of them becomes downright suspicious," I said.

"Aimed at who? You, me, or Felicity?"

Before I could answer, she said, "It's preposterous that anyone would want to kill me." With a sulky pout, she added, "Or Felicity."

"I can't really think why anyone would want to kill me," I said slowly, "but perhaps there's more to my job here than meets the eye, at least someone thinks so."

"All you're doing is changing some menus," she said scornfully.

"True," I said, "but you must admit I'm doing it with a flair."

"That *is* all you're doing, isn't it? Changing menus?" She was pressing seriously now.

"Of course," I said, but she was eying me in a judgmental way.

When the others returned, she delivered a scathing attack on the unknown marksman. Her eyes flashed and her vocabulary was remarkable in its range—all the way from Anglo-Saxon expletives to current gutter slang. They looked taken aback at the onslaught and all denied having fired in our direction.

"Well, someone shot at us, and it must have been one of you careless idiots! We could have been killed."

They had a mini-inquest right on the spot, but it was inconclusive. In order to make sure they all had clear fields of fire, they had kept so far apart that they remained out of sight of one another. As a result, not one of them could act as an alibi for any other. There was nothing to suggest who fired the shot.

"Could it have been someone else?" asked Felicity. "Richard, could there be someone else in the grounds?"

"Hardly," he said.

"One of us would have seen him," Norman said.

We broke up. Norman and Neville took the pickup truck, which I noticed had a winch mounted behind the cab. They were to retrieve the deer. They had shot eight, they told us, which was the limit set by the Forestry Commission. The rest of us went back in the Land Rovers in uneasy silence.

One of the servants intercepted me as I entered the hall. He lowered his voice to cut down the volume—echoes rolled around the vast dome and came back down.

"Inspector Devlin would like a word with you, sir. She's in the billiard room."

I hadn't seen that part of the castle, so he told me where it was. The two billiard tables took up only a part of it, and the inspector had moved in two desks; constables sat at each with telephones and laptops. A paperless society might be the aim, but it had clearly not yet been achieved here as each man had stacks of what were presumably reports.

The inspector was sitting on a small, uncomfortable-looking chair at a clear desk. She was on another telephone, but grunted a few words and hung up. She regarded me with a baleful look. "Anything to tell me?" she rasped.

"I have just been watching the culling of the deer herd," I told her.

She didn't change her expression. I concluded that it was part of her normal repertoire and not aimed specifically at me.

"I was with Angela Harlington; we were by a clump of trees. A bullet hit a tree very near us."

She rapped out a series of questions: who was there? where was everyone? how far away? what could we see? She had the whole picture in two or three minutes. I was impressed by her ability to gather information rapidly and assemble it.

"What's your opinion? A deliberate attempt, or carelessness?"

"I don't know," I said. "I assume they are all experienced hunters, so carelessness seems unlikely. If it was deliberate, then who were they shooting at, and why?"

She kept her steady stare directed at me. "Is there something you're keeping back from me?" she asked sharply. "Are you sure you're only here for this business of changing the menus?"

It sounded like a very trivial pursuit, the way she put it. "Changing the menus is one of the missions that make up my job," I told her. "It may not sound very important to you but—"

She waved a hand dismissively. "But it is to you. Yes, all right. My question is, are you here for any other purpose?"

I could explain that Sir Gerald had asked me to stay on and see what I could find out about the death of Kenny Bryce, but I didn't think she would take kindly to the idea of my acting as the detective after I had assured her I was not. I stuck to the literal truth. "Inspector, I came here for one purpose only—to advise on the menus."

She cleared her throat. It served as a comment better than words but I didn't mind; it was getting me off the hook, or so I hoped.

"Nobody wants to shoot you, then?"

"I can't believe they do, no. Nor could I think of a reason why."

She shifted her body to an even more awkward position in the uncomfortable chair. "In that case, and if it was deliberate, then they were shooting at the girl."

"I don't know any reason for that, either."

"H'm," she grunted. "I'll talk to them all." I was a little surprised. I had thought she might dismiss it, but she added, "Coming after that bow and arrow business, we need to know more about it."

"You heard about that?"

"Lord Harlington told me. Just missed the other daughter."

I decided not to say that it just missed me, too. The less I said the better.

One of the constables came over. "Excuse me, Inspector, could you take this call? It's—" She cut him off with a chopping motion of one hand. It wouldn't do to let me hear who she was going to talk to.

I took the opportunity and said quickly, "I'll be gone this afternoon for a few hours. I'm having lunch with a former police officer, an old friend."

She hesitated, then nodded and went to take the call. I decided to get away before she could ask me anything further.

The London Heralds' Society is in the area known as the City. Most of the financial institutions are here, crammed into this relatively small area. Here banks, insurance companies, stockbrokers, and commodity exchanges conduct worldwide business; the society met on Throgmorton Street near the Bank of England.

Stone steps led up to highly polished wooden doors with large brass handles. I pushed a brass button and one door opened to reveal an elderly but dignified man in a smart uniform. I told him I was to meet Edgar Sampson here and he conducted me into a glass-walled cubicle where Edgar was already waiting.

We were both taken into an adjoining room. It was large, airy, and had a skylight that took up a major part of the ceiling. Shields and banners covered the walls, but they were widely spaced, minimizing ostentation. One half of the room was raised from the rest and on this half was a circular table with a shiny wooden top. A man sat there waiting for us. Edgar introduced me.

Francis Somerville was the Knight Pursuivant, I learned. It was one of the highest titles in the society, the purpose of which was to maintain the traditions of heraldic symbolism and aid persons in tracing their genealogical roots. He was a large man and his blue velvet jacket had been tailored for him before he had put on weight. His face was florid and his hair was white. His pudgy fingers fluttered as he talked through oversized white teeth. His voice was sonorous; he obviously loved being the center of attention.

Edgar buttered him up with a glowing description of his prominence in the field, then cleverly introduced me with a minimum number of words, ending with "This is a highly confidential investigation, you understand, Francis." That blocked the Knight Pursuivant from asking any questions and at the same time preempted his using similar phrasing to decline to tell us about the Harlington family. Not that any likelihood of that seemed probable—Francis Somerville liked to show off his knowledge, and once he was absolved of any suggestion of breaking confidences, he was only too ready to talk.

First, though, he insisted on taking us on a tour of the large room, pointing out the shields on the walls. They were carefully chosen, he explained, in order to show how shields tell the story of a family through generations. He pointed out the "tinctures," the name given to colors used in the coat of arms. Gold and silver were the most prominent, then came sanguine for blood, sable for black. Animals and birds featured extensively, particularly lions, wolves, and eagles.

"Heraldic symbols," he told us in his fruity voice, "developed in the Middle Ages with the use of armor. The suit of armor made it difficult to distinguish friend from foe during violent, hand-to-hand combat and knights developed heraldic symbols so that they could identify each other." He took us, step by step, through several of the shields on the wall, telling us of the significance of the symbol of a tower—the family home; three arrow-heads—a battle won by archers; a lion wearing a crown—loyalty to the king, which brought honors to the family.

I found it fascinating. Edgar listened with rapt attention even though he had obviously heard it all before. It was Edgar who thanked Francis for his exposition and then brought him gently back to the Harlington family.

We went up to a vast, highly polished table. Francis nodded to us to take places and he took an imposing chair with a red silk seat and intricately carved arms and back. He pulled forward a large leatherbound book that was lying on the table. He opened it at a tasseled bookmark. "This is the Harlington crest. It is a very old family. In the fourteenth century . . ." Edgar politely let him finish a couple of sentences, then eased him into the present.

"Oh, yes," Francis said in his rounded tones, "we don't dwell only in the past here, you know. We keep abreast of all of our families. Many are still prominent and successful today. Harlington is one of them. His father did a magnificent job of saving the castle when it was in danger of becoming a ruin after the Second World War, and the present Lord Harlington has continued that policy. The idea of having jousts and banquets and things—and letting hordes of people in every day—raised a few eyebrows at the beginning, as these things did in a few other landmark buildings. But Harlington Castle has been saved from decay and dilapidation and is preserved for posterity, for a few more decades at least."

"I have found Lord Harlington to be extremely friendly," I said. "I haven't met his wife, though. She doesn't seem to be around at all."

"Poor Sylvia. She'll never be able to take her place at the castle again, I'm afraid." He shook his white head sadly.

"I thought she was recuperating in a nursing home and coming home soon," I said.

"I doubt she'll ever be able to return," said Francis.

"Cancer, isn't it?" asked Edgar innocently.

"Yes, but her earlier affliction is more of a problem," Francis said. He looked from Edgar to me. "Terrible thing."

It was clear he wanted to tell us. We gave him a moment, then Edgar leaned forward. "Earlier affliction, Francis?"

"She is quite insane, poor woman."

"I didn't know that," Edgar said, appalled.

"Violently so," Francis added. "Very sad. Hereditary: her mother died in an institution. Lord Harlington's first wife died of cancer too, you know. The onset came very quickly, she died in six months."

"Yes, I remember," Edgar confirmed.

"Yes, Gerald did very well to take on two more children—though, of course, they were almost grownup by then." Francis saw my look of surprise. "Oh, didn't you know? Richard and Felicity were his children by his first wife, Marion. When Gerald married Sylvia, she already had Norman and Angela."

"I didn't know that," I admitted.

"I didn't either," said Edgar. "I've been out of touch with the family for some years."

"They seem to get along very well," I remarked.

"I believe so." Francis chatted on for some time, a fountain of knowledge about the aristocracy, royalty, and stately homes. Then he asked me casually, "Is he coping all right, Sir Gerald?"

"Coping? With the running of the castle and the jousts and all that, you mean?"

"Yes. It's an awful lot of work."

"He certainly seems to be. He's involved in everything. Knows what's going on."

Francis nodded imperturbably. It was Edgar, knowing him much better than I did, who said, "Why do you ask, Francis?"

The Knight Pursuivant drummed his fingers on the carved arm of his chair. He had what would have been, on another, a coy look. On him, it was a look of careful consideration as to whether this tidbit of knowledge could be entrusted to our small assembly.

Edgar leaned forward expectantly. "If it's something that will ease the task of our friend here," he began.

"We wouldn't want you to betray any confidences," I added. "On the other hand, I like Lord Harlington, and if there were any ways in which I could help him . . ."

"Under those circumstances, I am sure," said Francis in a pontifical tone, "that I am justified in telling you this. I don't doubt that you have his best interests at heart. Everybody who knows him feels the same way." He drummed his fingers again. Edgar still leaned forward expectantly. Francis nodded, sat back, and spoke.

"Lord Harlington has only six to twelve months to live."

"Good Heavens!" Edgar exclaimed. "Are you sure, Francis?"

The Knight Pursuivant turned on his reproving look. "His personal physician is one of our members here."

I felt a profound sadness. It was as if I had known the man much longer. Edgar straightened up, shook his head. "I really am sorry to hear that," he said. "I have only met him a few times but I liked him very much."

"As does everyone who meets him," said Francis.

We were outside when I said to Edgar, "Well, you were right. Hardly a sparrow falls from a battlement that Francis doesn't know about it."

"He's a great old gossip, isn't he? Thought you'd find it useful," said Edgar. "How about a drink?"

CHAPTER SEVENTEEN

We had two drinks. Edgar liked American-style martinis; I had gin and tonic. We went to "The Captain's," one of the numerous bars that sprang up during the peak of the Thatcher era to cater to the large numbers of prosperous yuppies who flocked into the City. Many of these establishments were like the one we were in, a remodeled underground wine cellar. The domed brick ceilings, the tiled floors, the hidden lighting, and the semiconspiratorial air of the whole place put one in mind of the Gunpowder Plot or a Cold War espionage rendezvous.

Most such places still thrive and some have added upscale eating facilities. This was one and we decided to eat. Edgar, not an adventurous eater, had a prawn cocktail and a grilled salmon steak. I had a tomato, arugula and ricotta salad, followed by lamb chops with a yogurt and mint marinade. The chops were grilled with most of the marinade still sticking to them. This place catered to a wide range of tastes.

Although it was still early, it was already crowded. Most customers were young men and women leaving their offices and their computers for the day and needing sustenance to face the hour or more train ride back home to the suburbs. Glistening faces, clattering glasses, shouted orders, snatches of conflicting conversations: these things made it an exciting place to be, although perhaps the financial arenas that most of them had just left were equally exciting.

———

The train back to Hertfordshire was just as crowded, but it left and arrived on time. At the castle, I went into the hall and spotted one of the young constables who had been with Inspector Devlin in the billiard room. I asked him to inform the inspector that I had returned, and as he nodded and walked away, I was accosted by an attractive young blonde. She greeted me with a smile. I returned it and told her how glad I was to see her.

She was Sergeant Winifred Fletcher of Scotland Yard's Food Squad, but she gave no clue of that affiliation. She was wearing a trim gray suit that fitted her to perfection and her hair looked as if she had just come from the beauty parlor. I complimented her on her appearance. "A perfect disguise. No one would ever suspect you of being a"—I looked around with a conspiratorial air—"a you-know person."

"Good. I wouldn't want to shatter your image by having people think you were a nose."

I knew that she and her superior, Inspector Hemingway, liked to throw Victorian underworld slang into the conversation occasionally, hence her use of the word for a police informer. We both paused as another constable walked past us without giving us a second glance. "You could get by anyway," I told her. "The place is full of jacks."

She smiled at the word for detectives. "Are they progressing?"

"You must know more about that than I do. As far as we civilians are concerned, Inspector Devlin did not learn sharing in school and hasn't picked up the virtue since."

Half a dozen Asians in shiny new suits that they must have bought the day before came across the floor, chattering happily. One of the servants passed, carrying a large envelope, and several businessmen, evidently here for the banquet, stopped to discuss some weighty matter of commerce. Winnie and I waited to see the flow of pedestrian traffic subside, then walked over to stand some distance away from the foot of the wide staircase. Here, we had a tiny oasis.

"Inspector Devlin has prevailed on the Chief Constable not to call in the Yard just yet. Lord Harlington has put on some pressure too; he doesn't want any wild press stories about the persons poisoned earlier. You probably saw the press release—it only referred to an unfortunate death. That suits us at the Food Squad fine. We all want to keep it that way. The forensic people are making further tests on boro-amine. The only item that has come out so far is that boro-amine in this form, whatever it is, contains a significant amount of vitamin K."

"Is it added for some reason? Can't imagine why, though."

She shook her head. "Doesn't seem like it. More probably it's an integral component."

"Does that tell us something?"

"If so, we don't know yet what it is."

"Well, I'll keep it in mind," I said. "It might fit in—somewhere."

"Anything new here?" she wanted to know.

I told her of the discrepancies I was finding in the castle's quality control of its suppliers. She seized upon the implication immediately.

"If their QC's lax, some dangerous ingredient might be present."

"Yes. The supplier of fish runs a very sloppy operation. But I have nothing definite on them. Meat seems okay, but I was suspicious of the bread." I told her of my visit to The Muffin Man and she spotted the trend of my thinking at once.

"Ergotism?"

"That's what I had in the back of my mind. Couldn't see any likelihood of it in the bakery, though."

"It would fit," Winnie said thoughtfully.

"It would fit your multiple poisoning investigation better than it does this much more specific case here. I think it's a dead end really—The Muffin Man seems like a well-run operation. Besides," I added, "there's something else."

"What's that?"

"Two more murder attempts."

Her lips parted in surprise. "Two more?"

"Maybe." I told her of the arrow and the gunshot. She looked even more surprised. "Just enough possibility of either one being accidental," she said, musing. "The odds are awfully long against two of them, though."

"I agree."

"You were with a different sister each time, you said?"

"Yes."

"What's your assessment of them?"

"They seem to be nice girls," I said, selecting a suitable cliché.

Winnie smiled. She had a powerful combination at her disposal—strong feminine intuition plus a natural instinct for detection. It was unfair. "Very attractive, too?"

"Yes, I suppose they are." It was pointless trying to fool Winnie.

"I'm glad to hear you're taking this assignment conscientiously," she said.

"I always do."

"Yes, but I mean you're spreading yourself around. You're with one sister when an arrow is shot at her and with the other when a rifle is fired at her."

"If they were," I amended.

"True," she agreed. "But then, being the common denominator, you will have considered the possibility that you were the target."

"Can't imagine why. No reason for anyone to be suspicious of me."

The smile returned. "Anything else?"

"I don't think so," I said.

"I have to go. We'll be in touch." Her heels clicked on the marble floor and she was just going out of the door when Don McCartney appeared at my shoulder.

"Good-looking woman," he commented. "Is she a tourist?"

"Said something about being from Scotland."

Well, it was half the truth.

He watched her exit with appreciation, then turned to me. "I wanted to have a word with you," he said. "We have a couple of events coming up. First, we have the Battle of Moreston Marsh. We put this on every year. It's a reenactment of one of the crucial battles in the history of Harlington Castle. It's a stirring spectacle—I know you'll enjoy it. Local historical societies and others participate; so do our own people—the stuntmen and so on. We put on a banquet for them all afterwards. Victor probably has it largely planned, but you might want to talk to him about it."

"I will," I said. "You mentioned two events?"

"Yes. The Empire Historical Association is coming next month. There'll be about two hundred of them. We'd like to put on a really special banquet for them. You know what I mean—really unusual, genuinely medieval, but at the same time top quality."

"No budget restriction?" I asked.

"No," he said, then laughed. "Well, within reason, of course. Hope you've got some brilliant ideas."

"Shouldn't be a problem," I told him. "Have you told Victor Gontier about this yet?"

"He will have had a memo but he may not have done anything about it yet. There's plenty of time."

"I'll have a chat with him," I said.

CHAPTER EIGHTEEN

McCartney left and I heard a voice calling me. It was Lord Harlington. He looked very casual in a cream sweater and slacks. He had the same look of tension that I had noted before, but I assumed that it was from the many burdens of the rich.

"Been in the city, I hear," was his opening.

There was no way he could know I actually had been in the City and I had to presume he merely meant London.

"Making a few inquiries," I said lightly. After all, I could hardly tell him that I had been investigating his family tree.

"Any progress?"

"Possibly," I told him, trying to blend a cautious optimism with a hint of revelations to follow. But not now.

A party of Germans went by, unaware of their proximity to a real lord. We moved aside to let them pass without having to break ranks. They were planning their next day and saying unkind things about the English weather.

"You must mind these hordes of people wandering about through your house," I said. "Trampling all over your estate, destroying your privacy."

He shrugged. "From a practical viewpoint, if I didn't open Harlington Castle to the public, I wouldn't be able to own it. I may be confined to one wing, but that's better than a flat in Bayswater. We need an income of twenty-five thousand pounds a year just to control the woodworm. Some of the other figures relating to the estate would astound you."

"I don't doubt it," I said.

"Besides," he went on, "if one has the good fortune to live in such a beautiful place as this, then surely its beauties, its history, and its traditions should be shared."

"I agree with the sentiment, but there must be times when you feel resentful."

"Living anachronistically in one wing of a vast palace is not necessarily rewarding to the soul or comforting to the body. But as a nation, we are great ancestor worshippers . . ."

Was there something in his tone that hinted he knew the reason for my visit to London? I felt uneasy. I liked Lord Harlington and sympathized with his predicament. I wouldn't want him to think I had been spying on guarded family matters that were none of my business. Then I told myself that there had been one suspicious death and two more attempts, so it was hard to be sure which incidents were my business and which were not. Anyway, he had been the one to suggest my staying on and investigating.

". . . as you must agree. To have generations of known forebears is a matter of great pride, even if a few of them were rogues and tyrants." He permitted himself a gentle smile. "To look at a portrait on the walls here at the castle and know that the subject stood in that same spot centuries earlier can be strangely reassuring."

"And know that they faced many of the same problems you face and found themselves in the same dilemmas."

"Exactly." He nodded. "Although, to be honest, our problems today are relatively minor. We don't face imminent attack by a jealous neighbor or some upstart count with a couple of thousand plunder-hungry ruffians and a few farm-built siege weapons. Nor do we have the threat of the Black Death killing a third of the population, without any idea of what causes it or how to stop it." He was about to go on but caught himself. He repeated that same likable smile. "You'll have to excuse me. I get carried away talking about this place."

"I can understand it," I assured him. "It's a magnificent edifice, and you've gone far beyond that with the jousts, the banquets, the tours, the entertainment, and so on. You've also done a remarkable job of combining two objectives which must often be conflicting. You've kept the place for your own enjoyment and satisfaction, and at the same time, you share it with others."

"And determined to keep it that way. Yes, we do have a successful operation here, a lot of good people to run it, and a financial situation that many a corporation might envy."

I wondered if there was something behind those words, especially the last ones. One way to find out—well, find out something anyway.

"I don't suppose it's very likely that a competitor in the business would be behind the happenings here?"

He shook his head firmly. "The thought had occurred, naturally. But no, it's just too bizarre. Lord Montague or the Earl of Snowfell trying to bankrupt us so they take away our clientele?" He chuckled. "There must be a better word than 'bizarre' even."

"Too much like an Ealing comedy with Alec Guinness?" I suggested.

His chuckle ended and he said reflectively, "Well, after all, one of Alec Guinness's films did involve killing off eight relatives, didn't it?"

"Something like that. But surely, competition between castles isn't like companies battling to be first with a new fiberoptic or a diet pill?"

"No, no, of course not. No, not by any means. We're all good friends, all members of the same groups, all tied in with the National Trust"—he laughed lightly—"and all customers of the same few banks." That seemed to eliminate one improbable explanation that I had felt was hardly a realistic contender.

His Lordship was by no means the effete aristocrat he might occasionally appear to be, as I now found out. He fixed me with a piercing look and asked, "When I asked you if you were making any progress, your reply was, 'Possibly.' Would you care to amplify that?"

I tried not to show any hesitation before answering. "I have a number of loose ends. I am trying to determine which of them lead somewhere and which mean nothing. In the next few days, I expect to be able to do that. In the meantime, I am doing a one hundred percent job of updating the medieval meals."

He nodded. "Good." He didn't seem too disappointed that I hadn't told him anything. "Has Don told you about the forthcoming battle?"

"Just a few minutes ago. I told him I'd talk to Victor about it. Don also mentioned the impending visit of the Empire Historical people. I said I'd go over some ideas on that."

"Excellent. Ah—" He broke off as he caught sight of someone across the hall. "Well, good luck with your efforts and keep me informed." It was a dismissal and I accepted it.

We parted. Some distance away, I paused and looked back. The person he was now engaged in greeting was evidently someone he knew very well. She was smart and elegant, probably about fifty, and had a sparkling smile. Why did she look familiar? Then I remembered—she was the woman I had seen entering the castle upon my return from my excursion to London. A member of another aristocratic family, I wondered?

I watched them walk off, close together, her hand on his arm.

Have you seen Daddy?"

I turned to see Felicity. She was wearing a plain suit in a creamy color with black trim. At least, it would have been plain on many women, but it made her look particularly desirable. I could have complimented her on it but that became entwined with an immediate riposte along the lines of "I just saw him walk off with a very attractive woman," so I said only, "He left me just a minute ago."

"Oh, all right. I'll find him later. I wanted to ask him if the music room is ready for tomorrow night."

"A concert?"

"Not really. We rent it to groups in the neighborhood. Tomorrow is a rehearsal for a quartet playing Baroque music."

"I didn't know you had a music room," I said. "You have nearly everything else, though."

She looked at me in an appraising way. "Like to see it?"

"Of course."

She led the way up the staircase to the next floor and along a corridor lined with oil paintings, dark brown portraits of ancestors and sylvan scenes in green and ochre.

We went into a large room with paneled walls, heavy curtains, and two huge chandeliers. "Bit bright, aren't they?" she said, and turned a dimmer. The room was not musty but gave the impression that it was not used much.

There was enough light to reveal walls hung with ancient instruments. Music stands littered the floor and racks of scores covered one wall. Huge illuminated service books in leather and gilt lined the bookshelves.

"They had nothing like an orchestra in the Middle Ages," Felicity said. "They did play 'in concert,' though."

"Explain to me the difference," I invited.

"Well, music and song went together much more then. A group of stringed instruments would accompany a voice, then the wind players would do likewise, then perhaps the brass."

"How would they sound to us today?" I wondered.

Felicity smiled and shook her head. "Not very pleasing." She pointed to a large oil painting. "They are playing instruments of the time. That's a rebeck on the end." It looked like a swollen viola. "Next is a psaltery, it's a kind of zither. The shawm is an early oboe and the other one is a gittern—a forerunner of the guitar."

"Is that a bagpipe on the wall?" I asked.

"Yes. It's a very old instrument. The Romans played it." She reeled off the names of other instruments, some strange-looking but most obvious forebears of today's musicmakers.

She looked around in indignation. "Not a thing done in here. Look at it!"

"What do you want where?" I asked.

We soon had it the way she wanted it, the stands lined up in place and chairs positioned. I did most of the physical moving as Felicity sank into an S-shaped chair. She leaned back with a voluptuous sigh and patted the chair. "Know what they call this?"

I sat in the other half. Our hands touched. "A love seat," I said, "but I could never understand why. You sit in one half and I'm in the other half. Isn't that making the whole process unnecessarily difficult?"

Her chin rose. She looked very patrician in profile. "Difficulties were made to be overcome," she said loftily.

I reached over the barrier between us. She turned and leaned toward me. "A partial solution," I said a few minutes later. "Not wholly satisfactory, though."

"There's another piece of furniture over there," she murmured. I didn't look to see what it was. I let her take me over to wherever and whatever . . .

I wondered if sweeter music had ever filled that room.

CHAPTER NINETEEN

Gontier was in a harassed mood when I approached him. He tried to shrug me off with a "too busy right now but perhaps tomorrow" attitude, so I had to introduce pressure by name-dropping. Don McCartney's name produced only a mild reaction, but Sir Gerald's did the trick. I confirmed first that he had the menu already planned for the banquet after the upcoming Battle of Moreston Marsh. He did, and we went over it and I made a few suggestions. It was to be quite a formal affair as a number of local people, prominent in one way or another, always attended. Consequently, the theme of the meal, while suitably medieval, was not too dramatically radical.

Don McCartney had also told him of the forthcoming visit of the Empire Historical buffs. I added a doctored version of my conversation with Lord Harlington, emphasizing that, for this, we really needed to dig deep into Middle Ages cuisine. We went into the kitchen office.

"The first thought I had," I told him, "is from the English nursery rhyme, I wonder if you know it? 'Four and twenty blackbirds, baked in a pie' is how the first line goes. This was in fact a popular feature of medieval banquets."

He looked at me, a tinge of horror creeping across his face. "Blackbirds?" he murmured.

I could have reminded him of the popular and still repeated English belief that the French will eat anything that flies, walks, crawls, or swims. Such a catalogue would easily encompass blackbirds, making his look seem both superfluous and hypocritical.

Knowing that such an attitude would serve no purpose, I held my tongue on that score and explained.

"What they did was to bake an enormous pie, then make a separate false crust to place on top. The pie was cooked in the normal manner. Then, just before serving, twenty-four blackbirds were placed on top and the false crust pressed into place. When it was broken, out came the birds, to everyone's astonishment."

His expression was not encouraging. "I think I may have heard of that," he admitted. "I thought the blackbirds were in the pie to be eaten."

So there was substance in the English belief concerning French tastes after all. I said, "Most people think that, taking the line literally. But, you see, the birds weren't eaten—because the rest of the rhyme continues, 'When the pie was opened, the birds began to sing.' That means that they couldn't have met with death by baking. They flew out, of course, and then the real pie beneath was cut."

He was warming to the idea slowly.

"I don't think I've heard of any chef preparing such a dish today."

"Good," I said promptly. "It will be new to everybody."

"Still, I don't think we—"

"Let's go through the meal course by course," I suggested. "We can look at the problems later. In the Middle Ages, a banquet started with a salad."

"In France, we usually eat the salad at the end of the meal," said Gontier.

"True, but while we want to achieve historical authenticity, we also need to bend, even if unnoticeably, to modern tastes. Most of the guests on this occasion will be used to eating their salad first."

Gontier was in an argumentative mood this morning. "If you want to give them something different, one way is to serve the salad at the end."

"These guests will expect a sweet course at the end," I countered. "I am sure you can understand that. Wasn't it Louis the Fifteenth's court that served sweets after every course?"

He mumbled an acknowledgment of that and I moved on swiftly. "You are very fortunate here in having the Plantation. The salad can be made mainly of herbs, as it was in the Middle Ages, and you grow all your own. This type of salad can be disappointing when made with dried herbs."

He couldn't find any objection there. I continued: "Watercress, leeks, scallions, fennel, parsley, rosemary, mint, sage, and thyme would be excellent. A simple dressing of olive oil and wine vinegar could be added just before serving."

"Simple is often best," he conceded, and made a note. In order to cajole him into cooperating still further, I asked his opinion.

"As you know, it was customary to put everything on the table at once in those days. It was only in Victorian times that *service à la Russe* was introduced and the meal was broken up into courses. What do you think?"

I had already decided on my own stance, but I knew I had a fifty-fifty chance of getting his agreement. If I didn't get it, I had another argument to face. Fortunately, he said, "I think guests today are firmly in the habit of eating meals in separate courses. It is better to keep it that way."

He gave me a provocative look that challenged me to dispute him. I made a show of considering his point, then said, "You're right. I had thought that perhaps we—but no, you're right. Separate courses it shall be."

Our meeting progressed a little more smoothly after that. We debated at some length the ingredients of the soup for the next course. "In medieval times, soup was a big dish of fish or meat boiled with vegetables," I reminded Gontier. "We don't want to have a soup that would be out of harmony with the rest of the meal."

"Something lighter," he said.

"But not a consommé, I don't think. People feel cheated when they are given a clear soup. They prefer soups with content, with meaning."

He thought about that for a moment. "You are right. They do."

"One of the most popular soups at banquets used to be mussel soup," I said, "but not everybody likes mussels."

He shook his head firmly. "Not mussels. Perhaps a *soupe au pistou?*"

"Good idea. The Provence style, you think, rather than the Genoese?"

"Yes," he said. "Beans, potatoes, leeks, garlic, and tomatoes."

We put the soup on the list. A fish dish had to follow and we agreed on Thames whitebait, cooked fresh and crunchy. "A more substantial fish dish as well, you think?" he asked. "Perhaps salmon steaks?"

I was not sure that the dubious Seven Seas operation could be relied on, but this was no time to introduce that fly in the ointment and there were plenty of other fish suppliers, so I simply agreed.

Three main courses would come next. A spit-roasted baron of beef would be the star attraction, and suitably garbed page boys could do the basting as the beef turned slowly in the huge fireplace in the dining room. "Page girls," suggested Gontier thoughtfully and I concurred enthusiastically.

So that non-beef eaters could be accommodated, we proposed ham with Madeira sauce. Oven-browned potatoes, rice, and pasta would all be on the table. Vegetables from the Plantation would be available, of course, and then we came back to the pie that had started it all. Gontier was amenable to this idea by now. "Pigeons were used in those pies, weren't they?" he asked. "I don't think we want to use them."

"They were used but I agree we should leave them out. We could use chicken instead, couldn't we?"

He nodded. "Fried bacon would help," he added, "and we have excellent mushrooms from the Plantation. We should put those in."

"Right," I said. "Raisins were a common ingredient, too. Season with cloves"—I caught myself just in time and added—"and of course whatever other seasonings you think are appropriate."

"White wine and butter will be sufficient for the liquid," he commented.

"Excellent. The crust is more of a problem, though," I reminded him. "Medieval cooks would have used a hot-water crust paste, but to suit the modern palate, a short crust would be crisper and have more taste."

"Madeleine is a very good pâtissière; she can do that. We'll set large tables," he went on. "Six or so. That will be more festive and friendly. We will need only six pies that way."

I expected him to complain about having to procure a hundred and forty-four blackbirds but he didn't. I had been ready to reduce the count. Maybe he figured that the guests would be too impressed by their exit from the pie to bother to count.

"Dessert," Gontier said finally. "They will expect some different desserts."

"We'll give them great desserts," I promised. "Quaking Pudding for a start."

Gontier frowned. "I don't know that. What is it?"

"It contained mainly cream and eggs. It was very popular because it was so rich while the two main ingredients made it very wobbly—hence the name. It also had white wine, sherry, and eggs."

He looked dubious. For a moment, I thought bringing up this dish had been a mistake. But then he nodded. "Yes, I can certainly look into that."

"Any other ideas for desserts?" I asked quickly.

"We should make use of the Plantation's fruit," he said.

"Absolutely. Have you ever run across chardequince?"

"I think so. It originated in regions where the fruit season was short. Excess fruit was cooked very slowly and for a very long time—isn't that the one?"

"That's it."

"It turns the fruit into a paste that keeps for months." He was getting enthusiastic now that he was recalling memories from long ago. "Quinces were the most popular fruit for making it, but apples and pears were used too—we have lots of those here. Sweet wine and honey sweetened it, and they added something spicy."

"Ginger, turmeric, and cinnamon were used, yes."

"We have lots of berries here." Finally, he was really into the spirit of the thing. "We bake a lot of pies with them, but maybe we could do something medieval?"

"You're really challenging me now," I told him. "In the Middle Ages, they ate berries fresh off the bushes. They didn't cook them as a rule. Still, I'm sure we can think of something."

We had a brief discussion of tableware. To be really authentic, we should just give every guest a knife, but we agreed that might be overdoing the authenticity. So forks were not invented until much later—would we get any complaints? We decided not.

Our meeting ended on considerably better terms than it had begun. As I left the kitchen office, I wondered if I could now make similar progress on the mystery hanging over the castle.

CHAPTER TWENTY

I strolled through the grounds, absorbing the fresh air and hoping it would stimulate the investigative glands. Either it was the wrong stimulant or there were no such glands. I knew there must be something I ought to be sleuthing but I had no idea what it was.

On a grassy area by the jousting arena, I spotted some figures moving, so I walked over to see what was happening. I approached four strapping young fellows in leather pants and jackets. All had long swords and they were fighting in pairs. The blades clanged and clashed, swooping and darting in search of an opening. It looked very convincing except for the omission of any actual injury to any of them.

The pairs moved closer and closer together, then two of them backed into one another. They promptly switched opponents and resumed the contest. I watched them until they tired.

By then, half a dozen more similarly clad young men had arrived and were going into combat a dozen yards away. One pair consisted of a pike-wielding warrior and another with only a shield. Another pair was a swordsman against a fellow with a fearsome-looking two-handed ax. The others had long-bladed daggers.

I walked over to the original four, the swordsmen, who were sitting on the grass resting.

"Ever have an accident?" I asked. "Even by accident?"

One of them grinned and answered in a strong Birmingham accent, "No, we're all too good." The others laughed. One of them, clearly a Londoner, said, "This leather is a lot of protection, more than you might think. It would take a lot of the sting out of a strike, especially when you examine these closeup." He motioned to the swords and I looked at one of them lying on the grass. The tip had been rounded and the edges dulled.

"I recall reading somewhere that they boiled leather in those days," I said. "It would turn an arrow when properly hardened that way."

"I remember reading that, too," said another, a six-foot, fair-haired lad with a Somerset accent. "Good as chain mail it was, and a lot lighter."

"You look like you're getting ready to repel an invasion," I told them.

"The Battle of Moreston Marsh," the Birmingham boy said. "It's coming up in a couple of days. A mock battle, needless to say, but we're going to make it look good."

"Going to be here for it?" asked the fellow from London.

"I expect so," I said.

"Well, don't get alarmed when you see blood," said the fourth one. He had just enough of a singsong intonation to place him as being from Wales, and I now recognized him as Frank Morgan—the other stuntman, along with Kenny Bryce, who substituted for Richard Harlington as Sir Harry Mountmarchant. The rest chuckled.

"Blood?" I questioned. "Even when it's not mine, I don't like to see it."

"It's our own version of ketchup," the Somerset fellow explained. "Looks real even when you're close."

"Richard doesn't take part in that one too, does he?" I asked, keeping my tone casually light.

"He likes to," said London.

"But pressure's on him to stay out of it," added Birmingham.

"You think it's too dangerous for him?"

None of them answered at once. "There's no danger out here," said Frank Morgan slowly. "Kenny Bryce wasn't killed out here, was he?"

"Poisoned," London said. "That's nasty."

"Do they know how it happened?" I asked innocently.

Somerset shook his head. "Haven't heard. Kenny was a friend of mine. No reason for anybody to kill him, so it must have been Richard who somebody didn't like."

"I wonder what the police think about them both having the same girlfriend?" said Birmingham.

Neither of the others commented but it caught my attention.

"I hadn't heard that," I said. I tried to use a tone that invited more spicy confidences.

"It was a while ago that Kenny went out with her," Birmingham said.

"But she'd already started going with Richard, hadn't she?" London asked.

Wales was looking at me with a tinge of suspicion.

"Not a plainclothes policeman, are you?"

I laughed at such a ridiculous thought. "I'm just here for a few days. Working in the kitchen. Sort of updating it."

It appeared to satisfy them.

"I heard somebody talking about it possibly being an accident?" I said, still angling.

"Food poisoning, somebody said it might be." The contribution came from Birmingham. "Maybe it was something he was allergic to. That can happen. Heard of a fellow in Aston who died that way. They thought it might be something in the fish and chips he'd eaten."

London looked skeptical. "Hadn't he ever eaten fish and chips before?"

"Yes, but it was a different fish," said Birmingham.

I had a fleeting concern about the Seven Seas operation. Perhaps that needed further investigation.

Somerset was waving to someone behind me. The others were looking in that direction, too. I turned. It was Angela.

She was wearing a flimsy summer dress in periwinkle blue.

Her black hair was even more shiny in the sunlight and her large dark eyes seemed as active as ever in the smooth-skinned face. She acknowledged every one of the stuntmen by name as they all gazed at her admiringly.

"Thinking of volunteering for the pike brigade?" she asked me with a slight challenge in her voice.

"Wouldn't dare to tackle any of these fellows," I said. "With a brigade of men like these, King Harold would have driven William the Conqueror back into the Channel and history would be different."

"Where were you last night, Martin?" she asked the tall, fair-haired one with the Somerset accent. "Thought I'd see you in the restaurant after dinner." She struck a provocative pose with one hip thrust forward.

He grinned self-consciously. "Didn't see you. I went into the village."

"Better-looking girls there?"

"None better looking than you, Angela," he retorted. But she had already turned to Will, from Birmingham. "Maybe I'll see you tonight, Will. What happened to that moonlight stroll you promised me?"

"I'll be there," he said eagerly. "Even if I have to bring my own moonlight."

The others set up a chorus of catcalls and they all laughed.

"Will's not the only one with moonlight," came the soft sing-song voice from Wales.

"Is that right, Frank?" Angela's voice was a tiny bit contemptuous. "Do you have some, too? Or is yours more like moonshine?"

More laughs came.

"Sorry, Angela," said London. He picked up his sword. "But it's back to work. Got to get these ragamuffins into training to fight those rebels."

The others reluctantly picked up their weapons and once again the air rang with the clash of steel on steel. Angela sauntered over, not looking at me but watching the swordsmen. "They're good, aren't they?"

"They certainly are. Very expert. It must take as much training to avoid lopping off a man's arm as it does to do it."

"Weapons fascinate men, don't they?"

"Yes," I admitted. "They do. I suppose the more primitive weapons like these bring out the baser instincts."

"I haven't taken you on a tour of the armory yet, have I?" She was still watching the mock battle.

"I would certainly have remembered if you had—but no, you haven't."

"I'll have to do that very soon," she murmured and drifted away like a blue wraith, her gaze still on the combatants.

I contemplated the latest tidbit of information as I walked back toward the castle.

So Kenny had been a boyfriend of Jean Arkwright, too. Would Richard have been jealous of him? The answer to that would seem to be a resounding affirmative. A blueblood of Richard's caliber would surely feel jealousy more deeply than normal, for there would be an innate feeling that no commoner should have the gall to challenge a nobleman.

Or had I read too much Sir Walter Scott as a boy? Perhaps twentieth-century democracy and the principle of the equality of man had long buried such preposterous sentiments.

I didn't see Richard as the poisoning type, though. He seemed more likely to walk right up to Kenny and punch him in the face. Still, my friend Winnie Fletcher, on Scotland Yard's Food Squad and no stranger to death, had told me more than once that "almost anyone can commit murder."

CHAPTER TWENTY-ONE

I left the dining area just in time to see The Muffin Man's van pulling out of the driveway. I wondered idly if he made two deliveries a day. It was customary for a bakery to deliver early in the morning while the bread was still fresh.

I didn't go away, though. I hung around outside the cafeteria, waiting for the warriors I had been watching. As they were still hard at their task when I left, I presumed they would be eating on the second shift. Sure enough, they showed up in about fifteen minutes. They appeared glowing in health from their activities and not as much as one limb seemed to be missing.

They were in small groups, which suited me fine. Frank was there with Alec from London and Martin from Somerset. I intercepted them as they approached.

"No accidents, I'm glad to see."

Alec grinned. "We've had a lot of practice. Can't afford mistakes."

I looked at the Welshman. "Frank, can I have a few words with you?"

"I suppose so." He didn't seem too surprised.

Alec said, "See you later, Frank." He and Martin from Somerset went on into the cafeteria.

"How about if we talk over lunch?" I suggested.

"Suits me," he said agreeably.

After a careful survey of what was on offer, I selected a tomato salad, a bowl of carrot and lentil soup, and a sandwich of salt beef with horseradish sauce. I don't eat gourmet every meal and believe that, in this way, I enjoy those I do eat all the more. A glass of sparkling water made a suitable accompaniment and I wondered idly what would be on the menu that evening.

"You'll need to eat more heartily than me," I told him. "All that exertion must burn off a lot of calories."

"Never have a weight problem." He took a bowl of potato and carrot soup; a sirloin steak with onions, mashed potatoes, green beans; and a slice of chocolate cake. He poured a cup of coffee and added plenty of sugar and milk. "Keep me going till dinner," he grinned.

He had the typically dark Welsh features, curly black hair and bright blue eyes. Some Welsh look swarthily Gypsy, a similar strain to those known as "Black Irish," but Frank Morgan was more open and friendly. Until now, he hadn't even been curious about why I should want to talk to him away from the others.

"I suppose you're wondering why I wanted to talk to you," I said.

"After three police interrogations, I'm getting used to it."

"It was you out of your group of four who asked me if I was a plainclothes policeman," I reminded him.

"I did—and you said you weren't."

He was scooping up the soup as if he were famished. I assumed that he was. I had had time while standing, waiting outside the cafeteria, to prepare my approach and I didn't intend to rush it. I picked at my salad, enjoying it but eating a small piece at a time.

"That was true. I am not a policeman. Not plainclothes or any other kind."

He paused in his demolition of the soup, looked at me, nodded, then resumed scooping. I went on too.

"I told you I was working with the kitchen people. That was true. What I am doing is helping to rework the food being served in the medieval banquets. Make them more medieval but keep them authentic and even tastier if possible."

He finished the soup, pushed it away, and began on the steak. It didn't stand a chance.

I continued. "As there is a suspicion that Kenny Bryce was poisoned, the police have talked to me on several occasions. I am a food specialist; it was understandable that the police would want to talk to me."

I paused, pleased by how close I was managing to keep to the truth.

"I can hardly expect to uncover any information that the police don't have already, but I was with Kenny when he came into the tent. He was already suffering intensely. I stayed with him until he was taken to the hospital. So I feel a certain involvement. Does that make sense?"

He completed the dispatch of a large quantity of mashed potatoes. "Sure."

"You and Kenny both played Sir Harry Mountmarchant along with Richard Harlington, didn't you?"

"Right."

"So you knew Kenny well?"

"Pretty well."

"You know Richard, too?"

"Yes."

"I understand that Richard always ate a salad before he went out to do battle with the Black Knight."

Frank cut another huge piece of steak, made sure it was amply loaded with onions, and put it in his mouth. It was not surprising that his answer was a nod.

"From the buffet," I added.

He kept chewing. The steak looked very tender and I wondered if that much chewing was an excellent habit acquired in childhood or if he was stalling with his answer.

He had to finish eventually. I waited with patience.

"That's right," he said.

"You see the point here, Frank. If Kenny ate anything that Richard should have eaten, that may be how the poison was administered. Of course, if it came from the buffet, that makes it very unlikely. Others would have been poisoned too in that case."

He cleaned his plate and drank most of the coffee.

"It looks that way, right."

"I'm sure you told all this to the police," I said.

"All of it."

"You knew Kenny and you know Richard. There might be some little thing that you didn't think of when you talked to the police. Was there? Anything at all? Now that you think about it more?"

He pulled the cake closer and reached for a fork.

"Can't think of anything."

I had only one more card to play.

"You say that you know Richard. Do you consider him a friend?"

The question took him unawares. "Well, yes—as much as he can be. I mean, he's the son of a lord and—"

"Frank, you must know that if someone wanted to kill Richard and killed Kenny by mistake, they might try again. Next time, they might succeed. Richard's life may be in very grave danger."

His full attention was on the cake. It looked as if four mouthfuls might do it.

"I don't want that to happen. I'm sure you don't either. Let me know if you think of anything. Or tell the police. Or even both."

He finished the cake. He looked at me. "It's hard to believe."

"I know it is. Events like this don't normally happen in life. But this one has happened."

He reached for the coffee cup again, although I suspected it was empty. "There is one thing," he said. "One time, when Kenny was replacing Richard, I was walking through the cafeteria with him and he stopped and took a salad, carefully wrapped, from the back shelf of the cooler. Kenny must have been with Richard and seen him do that—I suppose one of Richard's girlfriends in the kitchen made it for him. Kenny grinned and said, 'If I'm replacing him, why shouldn't I eat his salad?' "

"If Kenny did that once, he might have done it again," I said slowly. "And it might have killed him."

"I don't know anything about that," Frank said doggedly. "I only saw it that once."

By now the cafeteria was filling up. A girl in a kitchen uniform came to the table.

"Hello, Frank," she greeted him warmly. "Enjoy your lunch? We'll be putting out pork chops tomorrow, your favorite." She had blond curls and a bright smile.

He nodded, drank the cold dregs of the coffee, stood up, and left.

I thought I had accomplished something but the result would be like a soufflé—only time would tell.

It occurred to me that this was a good time to intercept people. They all ate at approximately the same time and all could be encountered either entering or leaving the various eating areas. I couldn't think of anyone else leaving the cafeteria whom I might want to talk to, so I decided to try the dining room.

The theory was working. There was Felicity just leaving.

"Eating some of your own produce, I'm sure. How was it?"

She smiled pleasantly, making no effort to refer to the last time we had been together. She was wearing a silky blouse in a sunflower yellow color and a skirt a few shades darker. "It was good—as it usually is. I had prawns in an Indian-type sauce, Jalfrezi, I think it was called. They were not from the Plantation of course, but everything else was—the duchesse potatoes, the lima beans and the grilled tomato."

"Sounds tasteful."

"They do a good job there." We walked along together. "Speaking of jobs, how is yours progressing?"

"Coming along," I said. "Victor and I have the menu worked out for the banquet after the battle on the marsh. This Empire

Society banquet, later, is presenting some intriguing possibilities. We're hoping to be really unusual and bring out a few surprises."

"Yes, I'm looking forward to that too," Felicity said.

"Do you get to attend all the banquets here?"

"Oh no, not all. But I was roped in as a patron on this one—or maybe it's a benefactor. I get a lot of those posts, can't always remember which is which."

We paused at the turn that went to the castle. We waited as a vehicle went past us and I noticed the name on its side: "Newmarket Brewery Supplies," it said.

"Is it making deliveries here?" I asked Felicity.

"Yes, to our brewery."

"Your brewery? I didn't know you had one."

"It's only a small one, just enough for our own needs. We used to have a winery, did you know that?"

"I certainly didn't," I admitted.

"We did. It was here centuries ago, then a blight killed off all the vines and the winery went out of business. There were a few tries at reestablishing it but all without success. The winery had made mead, though, and that business continued. After World War Two, when the castle was being repaired and refurbished, the possibility of starting up a vineyard again was considered. But it was decided that the soil wasn't good enough so the buildings were turned into a brewery instead."

"You mentioned mead. I noticed how popular it is at the banquets. So you still make it?"

"Oh yes, we brew all our own."

"Fascinating," I told her. "Can I see?"

Her look was enigmatic. Was she thinking, "You know what happened the last time I showed you a part of the castle"? I wondered.

"I have a meeting of the Women's Institute this afternoon," she said with an enchanting smile, "but there's plenty of time. Come on."

CHAPTER TWENTY-TWO

K now much about brewing?" Felicity asked as we entered the squat stone building.

"I've visited a number of breweries in various countries and I'm familiar with their operations. I've probably been in more vineyards, though."

"You prefer wine to beer?"

"I like beer—real beer—but yes, I prefer wine. Like drinking it better than swimming in it, too."

Felicity turned her gaze to me. "That's an unusual practice. Why did you want to do that?"

"It wasn't deliberate. I fell into a vat in France a while ago."

"In the course of business?"

"Yes."

"Vinous espionage, was it? Seeking the secrets of Semillon?"

"It was red wine."

"Some people have lived for days on red wine."

"I wouldn't have on this occasion. I would have been in a bottle before then."

"That's taking wine snobbery to an extreme."

"In a way," I admitted. "Actually, I didn't fall—I was pushed."

"Ah, the classic alternates."

"It wasn't funny at the time," I told her. I probably sounded huffy. "The vats didn't have ladders inside and the walls were slippery."

"At least you couldn't die of thirst," Felicity said. She looked the other way as she said it, I suspect it was so that I wouldn't see her smile.

"I was rescued by a gendarme," I said.

"I'd like to hear the whole story sometime."

"I'll tell it to you. Sometime."

We went into the mead area. The air was heavy with sweetish fumes, thick and cloying, with a vaguely beerish aftersmell. A gnarled old fellow with a mahogany complexion met us. His features twisted into a genuinely pleased expression at the sight of Felicity. She introduced us. His name was Jim and he was the castle brewmaster.

"He's familiar with beermaking," Felicity told him. "More interested in mead. I said you know more about it than anybody else in Britain."

He cocked his head on one side. "Mead is probably the oldest alcoholic beverage known to man," he said. "Cave drawings in Valencia, made twenty thousand years ago, show two people collecting honey to make mead. When travelers to China—Marco Polo and others—finally reached the court of Kublai Khan, they were amazed to find magnificent silver fountains in the city squares. Each fountain had four spouts, all dispensing free refreshments to the populace. One spout served kumiss—the fermented mares' milk that the Mongols drank—another spout served wine, a third rice wine, and the fourth served mead."

I had expected Jim to have a country accent as gnarled as his face, but he spoke with the tones of an educated man.

"That's amazing," I said. "Do you use an old method of making it?"

"We could use sophisticated methods and modern equipment and turn out a pretty good brand of mead if we wanted," Jim said. "But people who come here expect to see everything medieval so we make mead the old way."

"And the old way is . . . ?"

"We use traditional oak casks. This is the size known as the firkin. It holds forty liters, or nine gallons." He pointed to a row of small wooden barrels stacked against the stone wall. "We make mead in batches of this amount. We have these vessels over here—they're stainless steel, but the finish makes them look like pewter so people think they're old. We put in thirty pounds of honey, a few handfuls of ginger, a few handfuls of dried elderflower, and fill with water. We bring it to a simmer and skim. We cool a little, stir in two kitchen ladles of active yeast, and let it sit overnight. There's your mead."

"Simple," I said, "and fast."

"There are some variations," Jim said. "We've tried adding egg whites—they make the liquid clear."

"Is that an advantage?" I asked.

"Most folk like it cloudy. They think it looks more authentic. Then rosemary alters the flavor slightly; so do cloves. We've tried those—and lots more besides—but we find the old recipe the best."

"You don't bottle any?"

"No," Jim said. "It's all consumed on the premises, draft only."

It was a small, compact operation. As Jim said, it could easily be commercialized. The visitors obviously liked it better this way, though—the rough wooden shelves with their canisters and boxes of ingredients, the lack of dials and modern equipment, and the supposedly pewter fermenting pots.

Jim was reaching for a mug and turning the spigot on a barrel. "Try one," he urged. "This is a bit fresh, needs a few more hours fermenting, but it gives you the idea."

It was sweetish but not objectionably so. It had a faintly beery taste.

"Reminds me of homemade ginger beer," I said.

"That can be made the same way. You just use more ginger, replacing the honey."

"How about cider?" I asked.

"We make that. We tried perry, too. That's the same as cider but made from pears instead of apples. It wasn't that popular, and besides, the pears we grow here are the eating kind and not really suited to perry."

"Jim knows better than to offer me mead," Felicity said.

"You don't like it?" I asked her.

"Never have. Give me a good Bordeaux any time."

"Like to see the beer-producing rooms?" Jim asked.

I had toured some microbreweries which are much more popular in the United States because the standard brews produced by the beer giants there are insipid, weak, and uninteresting. Fritz Maytag, the heir to the American washing machine empire, was a lover of good beer and resented the need to import it. He was the first to light the fire of revolution. Dissatisfied with the sameness and blandness of the routine beers, he bought the Anchor Brewing Company in San Francisco and started to make what came to be called "real beer."

This became the first of many. Today, supermarkets and liquor stores in the United States have a vast array of ales, beers, and stouts made by the microbreweries, plus an extraordinary number of imported beers.

I had been more interested in seeing mead produced, as that is a rare operation, but I wasn't going to turn down an opportunity to see a castle brewery making beer.

This one stopped me in midstride. It wasn't a medieval brewery but neither was it a slick modern microbrewery, either. "This is clever," I said to Felicity and Jim. "You've used copper throughout. Pipes, valves, pans, reaction vessels—everything. They give the place the look of the past but it clearly has the design and functionality of the present."

"That's what we aimed for," Jim said, pleased as Punch.

We walked on through. Even the dials and gauges were mounted inconspicuously in wooden cases, so they did not hit an incongruous note. Here and there, a wooden paddle, scoop, or crate added a further reminder of the past.

"We brew only two beers, a light and a dark," Jim told me.

"The dark is quite close to a real medieval brew, while the lighter one is closer to the modern taste. Both are top-fermented, moderate in alcohol content. We don't sell a lot but the operation is self-supporting."

"I heard some of the fellows in the cafeteria making remarks about your cider," I said.

"The cider is made over here." He led the way to a smaller room, a miniature version of the beer operation. "We don't make much any more. Our apple crop has been having some problems and we don't want to have to buy in apples."

"It's non-alcoholic, I believe," I said.

I glanced at Felicity. She rolled her eyes at the ceiling. The gesture of innocence was a sure sign of guilty knowledge.

"I suppose it's difficult to prevent an employee occasionally producing a few barrels of the alcoholic version," I said.

"I wouldn't be surprised," said Jim, keeping a straight face that gave it all away.

Outside, the air was light and fresh after the rich, heady atmosphere inside the brewing areas. We both breathed deeply.

"You may have to shower and change before joining the institute ladies," I told Felicity, "otherwise, they'll think you've been spending your time in questionable surroundings."

She shrugged. "That's all right. More than once, I've shown up at meetings with cow manure thick on my shoes."

"An excellent way to keep meetings short, I would think."

We were about to part when I said to her, "Is Richard taking part in the Battle of Moreston Marsh?"

"Yes."

"Do I detect an undertone of frustration in that word? Have you tried to dissuade him from taking part? Without success?"

She stopped walking. "I've tried and Daddy's tried. It's no good. He won't listen."

"Doesn't he consider himself in any danger?" I asked her.

"Oh, he trots out all the conventional replies, all the standard chauvinistic male statements. You know, life is full of dangers, he has his responsibilities to participate in these events, he's not going to be frightened off by an accident or two . . ."

"Is that what he considers these events to be? Accidents?"

"He refuses to think that anyone is trying to kill him and insists that Kenny could hardly have any enemies."

"The arrow that came between us? The gunshot that only just missed Angela and myself? What does he think about those?"

"Those can happen any time, he says."

"They can but they don't."

She sighed. "Well, I'll keep trying to get him to listen to reason. Meanwhile, I have to go."

"Tell the Women's Institute ladies to keep up the good work."

She smiled, then stood on tiptoe and gave me a kiss.

CHAPTER TWENTY-THREE

It was late afternoon and the kitchen would be starting preparations for the evening meals. I went to see how they were doing.

Madeleine was in charge. Victor Gontier, she said, was in the dining room and involved in a discussion relating to the wait staff. She was slicing strip steaks and told me they would be grilled medium rare in ridged pans and served with a relish of oregano, onions, and olives.

Sous-chefs and helpers were deep into various tedious but essential tasks. The inevitable chopping of potatoes, the trimming of asparagus, the julienne preparation of matchstick-thin carrots, and the cubing of pork loin for kabobs were underway. A tall, strong girl came in with a huge bowl of mussels and banged it down on a wooden bench.

Jars were being filled from central containers—chopped lemon zest, sprigs of mint, slivered almonds, shards of bittersweet chocolate, bayleaves, cheeseballs, dried cherries. They would not spoil or desiccate in the jars, for these were of a size to supply one evening's cooking only. It was highly likely also that many of these ingredients would never get their names on a menu, though their subtle influence on a flavor might well cause guests to frown, puzzled.

Madeleine gave a string of instructions to two of the sous-chefs, washed her hands, and came over to me as she wiped them dry.

"Victor and I have been doing some research on eels," she

told me enthusiastically. "Stewing in red wine was one of the earliest ways of cooking them."

"I believe so. A bit insipid though, don't you think?"

"I suppose they were. Then there were the eel pies you mentioned that they used to sell at fairs and at street markets. I looked up a few recipes for those—they might go well here."

I agreed. "They were cooked menagère style, weren't they?"

"Yes. Marinated in wine and spices, then fried in butter and put back into the marinade. They were put into the pie crust, layered with forcemeat with lots of chopped shallots and parsley, and baked. It's a good way of subduing the oily flavor—which is going to be the problem of matching it to modern taste."

"Exactly," I told her. "You've hit it on the head. That's why smoked eel is so good—the smoking removes the oily taste. But that limits its use. By the way, always make sure the eel is no longer moving."

She looked at me doubtfully as if she was not sure whether I was joking.

"They have a very slow nervous system," I said. "They will go on slithering around long after death. They have terrified many an old lady—not to mention nervous first-year student chefs."

"Like a turkey with its head chopped off."

"Right. Cutting them into short lengths will deprive them of their active tendencies. Personally, I think the Hungarian style of cooking eel is one of the best. You fry the pieces with butter and onion, then sprinkle with lots of paprika. You cover with white wine and cook a while. You remove the eel pieces, boil down the pan juices, and stir in cream. You pour this over the eel."

She nodded appreciatively. "That could be popular. Not too eel-like. Victor found some recipes for deep-frying in a light batter. That conceals their eely nature, too."

"Also any good thick and spicy sauce can be poured over them. Victor probably knows plenty of those."

"Oh, he does," she said confidently. "He's very good on sauces."

"Yet another way that used to be popular—and is tasty as well as authentically medieval—is to dip them in beaten egg and bread-crumbs and cook them on a skewer."

"That sounds old," she said. "We could cook them that way in the fireplace. Guests could watch."

We continued to discuss ways of making eel palatable and then went on to talk about frogs. Madeleine said that Victor knew a number of ways of preparing those, too. She was a bright girl and was growing more and more spirited over the challenge of pre-senting really medieval food. She admitted that the castle menus had been tailored too much in favor of easy modification.

I left the kitchen feeling more optimistic now that the level of cooperation was rising. As I came out, a servant in uniform was approaching, an elderly but spry castle retainer.

"Ah, yes, sir—they told me I might find you here. There's an urgent phone call for you." He handed me a cell phone. "Just leave it in the kitchen when you're finished."

A pleasant female voice greeted me. It had a vaguely familiar tone to it.

"This is Dr. Wyatt. We haven't exactly met but we have peo-ple—friends—in common. Listen, it's very important that we talk at once. I can't explain over the phone but it concerns events at the castle. I live in the village—Stony Stratton. Can you come here right away?"

The last sentence was couched as a question but it had a ring of authority that one might expect from a doctor. Even so, I was hesitant. She picked up on my hesitation. "It really is very ur-gent."

"All right. Where are you in the village?"

"Seventeen, Laurel Cottages. Do you know the village at all?"

"A little. I know the High Street and the Post Office."

"Laurel Cottages is a lane that runs off the High Street just past the Post Office."

"I'll be there," I said.

A shuttle bus was about to leave and I boarded, getting almost the last seat.

The shuttle bus stopped in what was called the village square. It was hardly big enough to merit the name, its main feature being the Church of St. Anselm which fronted onto it. It was just a small village church, but it had one unusual feature, one seen in just a few churches throughout England: a clock set into its façade. The time was a quarter to five. As I got off the bus, a blue van went by. It looked like the one I had seen at the castle. It slowed, and as the bus moved away, I saw the van stop on the other side of the High Street. I took a few paces so I could see just where. It was in front of a café-restaurant. The sign said "Roberto's."

It was flanked by a greengrocer's shop and a butcher's. Busy shoppers were going in and out. Adjoining the greengrocer's, the Ripon Arms was doing a modest trade.

While I was watching, a young man in an apron came out of Roberto's. The rear door of the van swung open from the inside and the young man lifted out a cardboard crate. He took it inside the café and the van drove down the street. I believed that solved one mystery. Now for another.

A phone box was in front of the pub. The Stony Strattonians were a law-abiding bunch—at least, they didn't vandalize their phone boxes. The thin phone book was neither torn nor battered. I opened it. Sure enough, there was a Dr. Evelyn Wyatt, and she did indeed live at Seventeen, Laurel Cottages, in Stony Stratton, Hertfordshire. So my precaution was unnecessary. But I had found myself in trouble before—trouble that could have been avoided if I had taken this same elementary step.

The lane called Laurel Cottages was clearly signposted—an ancient cobbled thoroughfare that might have accommodated horses but certainly not vehicular traffic. To make certain that this prohibition was clear, two heavy wrought-iron posts were set to bar anything other than pedestrians.

The cottages were upmarket versions of what were once called "workingmen's cottages," and still are in the estate agent business. All have been thoroughly modernized and are now quite expensive. The workingmen of a century ago would be turning over in their graves if they knew what their old homes were bringing.

Gardens in front blazed with flowers. Door knockers, handles, and letterboxes gleamed polished brass, and the mullioned windows were clean and sparkling. Number Seventeen was no exception.

I rang the bell. There was no reply. I tried again, still without reply. I looked up and down the street. No one was in sight. I tried the door and it opened. I stepped inside, feeling a slight shiver of apprehension.

I called out. All was quiet. I went on in, carefully leaving the door wide open.

The front parlor, as it would have been called in its heyday, was tastefully furnished without losing a period atmosphere. I went through into the next room. Books lined the walls, mostly massive medical tomes. Certificates and diplomas were hung behind a handsome carved desk with a green baize inset. File cabinets filled the rest of the space.

I called out again and there was still no answer. I went into the adjacent kitchen—and stopped. A woman was slumped over the table.

Her skin was still warm. I examined her quickly, but no signs of life remained. I leaned over her and inhaled. There was the faintest odor but it was sufficient. It was one I remembered.

In my business, I have to remember tastes and odors the way an insurance man has to remember actuarial tables and a bookmaker has to remember odds. I had only smelled this odor once before, but that had also been from a dead body—the body of Kenny Bryce.

The woman wore a dark blue sweater of light wool and a skirt in a tweedy pattern on a slim, trim figure. One arm lay across the table and her head was turned sideways alongside it. I bent down to look at her.

She was good-looking, probably in her late forties. She was familiar—but where? Then I recalled. I had seen her twice before, and both times she had been at Harlington Castle. She was the woman I had seen with Sir Gerald.

I checked for a pulse once more, then hurried to the study. Hadn't I seen a phone on the desk? Yes, there it was. I dialed nine-nine-nine and asked for the police.

A female voice answered on the first ring. I replied to all her crisp questions and was told to wait where I was, the police would be there. I hung up and had not moved when—

The doorbell rang.

CHAPTER TWENTY-FOUR

A uniformed police constable stood there.

I knew that the British police were wonderful, but this response must be a hot candidate for the *Guinness Book of Records*.

"You reported a disturbance here, sir?"

He was a youngish man, but he had been out of police training for enough years to view me with a careful mix of suspicion and caution.

"May I come in, sir?" He was already coming in before I could answer.

"Of course," I said. "You surprised me—"

"Yes, sir. Now perhaps you can tell me who you are—"

"No, I meant arriving so quickly. I had only just hung up the phone."

He looked me over, then his eyes swept through the room.

"We received the call about twenty minutes ago, sir. I was out at the hospital when it came in. I came here as quickly as I could."

"Not my call," I said, keeping as calm as I could.

"Ah, you called too, did you, sir?" I didn't like his tone of polite skepticism.

"Yes. You'd better come into the kitchen."

I led him into the kitchen. I heard him catch his breath as he saw the body. He wasn't that experienced, evidently, but he examined her efficiently.

"The lady's dead, sir," he said, standing up and not taking his eyes from me.

He took the cell phone from his breast pocket. His report was concise. He answered questions from a superior who was put on the line. He snapped off the phone.

"We'd better go into the other room. I'll have to ask you a few questions before the inspector gets here."

I knew the technique. Get a suspect or a witness to talk as soon after the event as possible. Compare their answers at that time to their answers to the same questions asked later. Pick on the slightest discrepancies.

The young constable did a competent job. I responded to his question about my presence, and he looked up when I said that I was temporarily at the castle.

"Ah, yes, having some trouble there, aren't they? Well, if you're there, you'll know Inspector Devlin."

I admitted the acquaintance.

"She'll be here in a few minutes," he told me. "We're lucky she's so close by."

I agreed how lucky we were.

The constable went on with his inquiries, digging deeper and deeper. All I learned was that the woman in the study was indeed Dr. Evelyn Wyatt and that this was her cottage. I didn't like some of his innuendoes—he didn't put them that way but that was what they were. Still, I kept my answers tight and simple. It was not that I had anything to hide, but I knew that when the redoubtable Inspector Maureen Devlin arrived, she would be asking me exactly the same questions—along with plenty of new ones.

An hour later, she was still asking. She had arrived after a few minutes, as predicted. Whether or not she would be in charge of this case, she didn't know yet, she said. But as she was in the immediate vicinity, she had been instructed to make a preliminary investigation.

She did it with the same cut-and-thrust style I had already become familiar with. She sounded as if she did not believe a word I said, and she would pound on the same point from different angles, sometimes making a case from one word.

When she had heard my story four times, I felt that she accepted it. Not enough to admit it by any means, but enough to get me off the hook. For the moment anyway.

I became more convinced of this as I gleaned fragments of information from her questions. The local police station had logged my call, but the reason the constable showed up so promptly was that they had received a call twenty minutes earlier. She avoided telling me whether it was a man or a woman, but someone describing him- or herself as "a neighbor" had reported hearing a suspicious noise from Number Seventeen. That was what the young constable had been investigating. It was why he had concluded his business at the hospital and taken twenty minutes to get here, and it was why he was so surprised at finding a dead body.

The distinct impression emerged that Inspector Devlin knew a lot about Dr. Wyatt. When I told the inspector of seeing the doctor twice at Harlington Castle, there were no queries concerning my knowledge as to why she might be there. I felt sure that the wily inspector knew. She wasn't out of questions, though.

"So you have never talked to Dr. Wyatt?"

I had told her that three times but I kept a tight rein on a sarcastic answer.

"That's right. I have never talked to her in the flesh."

"And when she phoned you today to ask you to come here, you weren't surprised to get such a call?"

"I had no reason to connect the woman who called me with the woman I had seen at the castle."

"Nevertheless, you weren't surprised?"

"Let's say I was puzzled but not dumbfounded. I came right away because I was curious."

"What did you expect to learn by coming here?"

"I had no idea. She told me she was a doctor but nothing else. I had no idea what to expect," I added to make the point clear.

She continued her patient and irritatingly repetitive interrogation. Finally, she came to the one query I had been waiting for. She didn't do so directly. She nodded as if satisfied and started to sit back with a body language that said she was finished. Then she rapped: "What connection is there between the doctor's death and the events at the castle?"

"I can't think of one," I said.

"Try. Try hard."

I paused for a few seconds so that she could see I was thinking. I had been turning over that very point in my mind ever since I had received the phone call, so it was no problem for me to say, "Absolutely none, Inspector. I can't think what connection there could be."

She studied me and her rawboned face hardened, if that were possible.

"If there is," she said, and her voice grew raspier, "I'm going to find it. So you'd better be telling me the truth."

I contented myself with the least of nods.

"We find you in a room with a dead body. You say you came in response to a phone call. You say you found the doctor dead when you got here. Someone else, a neighbor, had already called us to report a suspicious noise."

"Anonymous?" I asked.

She ignored that. I took it to be a yes. "We could take you into custody," she said, though I could detect no emotion in the statement, "but I'm going to let you return to Harlington Castle. You are still doing that medieval food business there, aren't you?"

Under other circumstances I would have hotly debated that description. I just said yes.

She stood. "You can go. I'll talk to you at the castle to-morrow."

I went. Quickly.

The dining room had the pleasure of my patronage that evening. Finding the dead body of Dr. Evelyn Wyatt had taken the edge off my appetite to say the least, but I had to eat. I wanted a meal beyond the limits of the cafeteria but decided against a repeat visit to the banquet room. The dining room filled the gap neatly.

A smoked eggplant salad provided a good start to the meal. For the main course, I chose the roast quail, stuffed with spinach and served on a bed of roasted leeks with wild rice and orzo pilaf. A guest nearby at the table had peppered lamb chops. They were accompanied by Idaho potatoes, braised in lemon-flavored chicken stock, then baked and lightly fried. Another had a walnut-crusted salmon fillet. With it came a sauce of garlic and cucumber whisked into yogurt.

It was very satisfying meal, even though I could not concentrate on it as it deserved. I am skeptical of coincidences so I found it hard to accept that the doctor's death did not fit somehow into the bizarre events at the castle. I had seen her here twice. Each time, she had been with Sir Gerald.

The fact that Sir Gerald's wife was in a nursing home and incurably insane was impossible to ignore. He was still an active and good-looking man, despite his years. Could there be a liaison between the doctor and Sir Gerald? But what might that have to do with the doctor's death?

I recalled Francis Somerville, Knight Pursuivant at the London Heralds' Society, who had told me that Sir Gerald had only months to live. Might that not make him all the more determined to enjoy the remainder of his life? Could the attractive doctor have been the way to do that?

A number of other lines of inquiry began to pop into my

mind. How to get answers to them? Sergeant Winnie Fletcher was the one to provide those, and I also needed to talk to her about her investigations to see if anything new had come up on the poisoning of the visitors to the castle.

I left the dining room and went to one of the public phones. I left a message for her to call me the next morning.

CHAPTER TWENTY-FIVE

When I was called to the phone, I hoped it would be my favorite detective sergeant from Scotland Yard, Winnie Fletcher. It was.

She said it was a Circle of Carème matter and hung up. That identified her—it was our prearranged code that came from the first time we had worked together. It also meant that I should call her back on a public phone on the chance that this line was tapped.

I went to a phone and called her. When she asked me if there was anything new, I said, "That depends on whether you keep up with suspicious deaths in surrounding villages."

"I don't like that condition," she said. "Tell me about it."

When I had finished telling her about Dr. Wyatt, she was silent for a moment. "But you never met her?" she said at length.

"No, I merely saw her."

"Do you think the same poison was the cause of death?"

"Superficially, yes, but I had no opportunity to make any kind of examination."

"In the light of other events surrounding the castle, an accident seems improbable."

I agreed.

"So, if it wasn't an accident, it sounds as if the doctor was murdered and someone wants you to appear guilty."

"It looks that way," I said.

"They must keep close tabs on your movements."

"That wouldn't be difficult here."

"Stony Stratton, you say?"

"That's right."

"I suppose Inspector Devlin was called in because she's so close?"

"She was—and she's very doubtful about me. It may be that only whatever good word Inspector Hemingway has been able to put in for me is all that has kept me out of the Bastille."

"H'mm." Winnie was weighing up police procedural considerations. "She will probably be given the case, with this connection of the poison. I'll call up the report after we've finished."

"I can't imagine what the connection means," I said, "but I'm inclined to think there is one. Meanwhile, did you have some news on your earlier poisoning reports?"

"Forensics have done more digging into boro-amine. They have reaffirmed its high content of vitamin K but don't yet know the significance. Inspector Devlin is looking into the habits of both Kenny Bryce and Richard Harlington—specifically whether they were, or are, vitamin consumers."

"An overdose?" I asked.

"Or a mistake? No, I don't think it was either one, but it's a point for you to be aware of."

"All right, I'll keep that in mind."

"Inspector Devlin hasn't made any suggestions about bringing charges against you yet, has she?"

"I don't like that 'yet,' " I objected. "No, she hasn't. I'm hoping I can continue to shelter under the umbrella of Inspector Hemingway. He'll protect me, won't he?"

"Coward. Inspector Devlin will probably keep this as an accidental death, just as she did with Kenny Bryce, until she accumulates more evidence. So she won't bring charges against you or anyone until then."

"It's really not cowardice," I told her. "It's complete innocence."

"The prisons are full of people who—"

"People who say that. You're a heartless sergeant," I told her. "It's a good thing you know me."

"If only we didn't need help so badly on this case," she said with an exaggerated sigh.

After I hung up, I headed for the library. I was almost there when I was intercepted by one of the young constables who were beginning to seem like permanent fixtures at the castle. He conducted me to a room I hadn't seen before. It had two constables, one male, one female, sitting at telephones. Inspector Devlin was at a desk across the room, which was large enough that we could not hear their conversations.

She invited me to sit, although the way she put it, it was more of an order. First of all, she went through the routine of my connection with Dr. Wyatt. I repeated what I had already told her four times at Seventeen, Laurel Cottages—that I did not know her, had never met her, had never spoken to her.

She went over all the other questions again. I gave her all the same answers as before. When she paused for a further barrage, I slipped in a question of my own.

"Was Kenny Bryce a patient of Dr. Wyatt?"

"What makes you ask that?" she rapped back.

"Seems reasonable," I said. "Likewise, Richard Harlington—was he a patient of hers too?"

She had undoubtedly considered those possibilities herself, and even if she had already found the answers, I knew she was not going to pass them on to me. Nor was she the kind of character to be sidetracked easily.

"For the time being, Dr. Wyatt's death is being handled as accidental," she told me in that raspy voice. "The facts that you were the one to find the doctor's body and you claim to have been there in response to a phone call from her are clouding issues. Which we will resolve very soon."

I nodded agreeably. She gave me a penetrating look.

"You can go."

I went.

I resumed my visit to the library. Lisa was there and she greeted me amiably. We chatted for a while about her duties and she told me how widely used the facilities here were.

"City libraries and historical societies all over call us for information," she said. "Especially about the earlier Middle Ages, which are not very well documented."

"You have books on a remarkable range of topics," I said, easing my way over to a set of shelves that I had already targeted. "These for instance"—I motioned—"books on plants and vegetables." I gave the impression of having been struck by a sudden thought. "These must have been a big help to Felicity with her Plantation."

"Oh, yes," Lisa said. "She spent a lot of time here. Still comes in often."

"You lend books out, I take it?"

Lisa shook her head. "No, we have people come here if they want to do research. If they know what they want, they write or fax or e-mail and we send back answers the same way."

"I noticed the empty space here," I told her with a smile.

She looked where I was pointing, then frowned. "That's strange. I hadn't noticed that. I wonder what book that is."

My experience of librarians was that the dedicated ones considered all their books as children and didn't like the idea of one of them straying from home. Librarians were also sticklers for detail and wanted to know where all their charges were at any time. Lisa seemed like such a person. She scanned the volumes on either side of the space.

"Hard to tell which one that is, I suppose." My words were hardly necessary to prod her into action. Her lips moved as she read the numbers on the spines of the books adjoining.

"I have my own system of numbering," she said. "I can tell very quickly which book is missing. I know it's not out on a table—I cleaned them all off this morning." She looked at me apologetically. "Oh, I'm sorry—can I help you with something first?"

"No, go ahead. This is fascinating."

She was clearly enjoying the demonstration of her system's efficiency. She twinkled fingers over her computer keyboard, went back to the shelves to check, twinkled again. She frowned, checked again, then came back to the keyboard and a title came up:

Poisonous Herbs and Plants.

We both looked at it. I felt a quickening of interest. I hadn't expected this. I looked at the name of the author: Clement Snodgrass.

"I know the name. Books by him are hard to find."

"He was well known in the eighteenth century," Lisa said. "He was an astrologer-physician. He set up an apothecary shop in Bishopsgate and wrote a book on the healing properties of plants. He had a huge collection of herbal remedies. The medical profession condemned him, of course, but he had a large following and helped a great many people. Then he felt it important to identify dangerous plants and herbs as well. That's why he wrote this book." She frowned again. "Now where on earth can that book be?"

I browsed a few more minutes to move the focus away from that particular book, then left. This was an unforeseen bonus. I had hoped at the most to get some generalities and here I had a specific.

I headed for the Plantation. A gardener was at work, pruning and weeding. He gave me a nod and I returned it.

I could hardly expect to uncover knowledge that dozens of police, backed up by immense technical resources, could not. The most I could do was to employ my expertise in a way that might not occur to them, to find some slender thread that the monolith of officialdom might overlook. It had been Winnie's reference to vitamin K that initiated my line of thought.

It was not rare for an amino acid to contain vitamin K, but it was certainly not common. An overdose of a vitamin supplement had seemed, at first, to be one idea to pursue, but the Plantation flashed through my mind because of vitamin K's association with plants. Leafy green vegetables all contain high amounts of that vitamin. The Plantation contained edible plants, herbs, and vegetables in abundance.

One other fragment of information surfaced at the same time. Richard was in the habit of eating a salad before he went out into the arena as Sir Harry Mountmarchant. On the day of Kenny's death, he had not done so. But any attempt at killing Richard by poisoning could not have killed Kenny as it would also have affected everyone else who took that same item from the salad buffet. Still, a large number of the ingredients of salads came from the Plantation. Did that mean something? In the case of Dr. Wyatt, all that had been on the kitchen table were a cup and saucer and a teapot.

I wandered through the Plantation. Among the leafy green vegetables were cabbages, lettuce, celery, leeks, spinach. I was looking for more when the gardener approached, hoe in hand.

"You keep all these looking remarkably healthy," I told him. He accepted the compliment with a nod. He was probably near seventy, lean and active, with a weathered, outdoor face.

"Lot of work," he said. "The healthier the plants, the more the birds, the insects, and the weeds like 'em."

"I'm sure. Have to use a lot of weedkiller, do you?"

He shook his head. "Do all weeding by hand. Miss Felicity don't believe in taking a chance with all them chemicals."

"That must make it very hard to keep the weeds under control."

"It does that."

"The same with the herbs, I suppose?" I said as we strolled to the herb and spice sector of the garden.

"Harder with them. Know anything about herbs?"

"A bit," I conceded.

"Soil that's been cultivated as long as this has here at the castle—well, it likes to come up with its own different varieties."

"Herbs from the past?"

"Aye, some of them. Betony, Solomon's seal, bloodroot, Jacob's ladder, owlsfoot—we've had 'em all."

I thanked him and wished him luck in his battle against garden intruders. I headed back to the library. Lisa was on the phone and I indicated by sign language that I was going to look at a book in the plant and herb section. She waved for me to help myself. I went to the shelf with the missing book and roamed along the titles. Another contemporary of Clement Snodgrass and Nicholas Culpeper was present: Luke Astridge. All three had been active at the time when earnest researchers were trying to merge—or separate—medicine, herbalism, physics, chemistry, and astrology.

I leafed through Astridge's book with its closely spaced lines and the occasional curlicued letters. I came to a section which dealt with poisonous plants. Owlsfoot, one of the dangerous plants that the gardener had mentioned, was listed. I suspected that in the missing book it had received more attention, but the paragraphs here were enough to give me a chill.

"Owlsfoot *(Allocca velenosa)*," I read.

Grows about two feet tall. Has a spike of blue flowers. Roots, stem, flowers and leaves are all extremely poisonous.

Symptoms. Dryness of the throat followed by tingling and numbness of the limbs, tongue, and throat. Loss of sensibility ensues swiftly along with dimming vision, muscular pains, slowed pulse, and violent convulsions.

Postmortem Appearances. No characteristics are evident. Death may be within one or two hours. One fiftieth of a grain can be fatal.

Treatment. No known treatment.

Toxicological Examination. Indeterminate. Edible members

of the aconite family such as horseradish are often confused with owlsfoot.

Other Characteristics. The plant is susceptible to variations in temperature and humidity. It may die and remain that way for years or even decades and then revive.

I finished reading and replaced the book. Here was the culprit. More modern books might have more up-to-date information, but owlsfoot had been deadly in the past and no doubt continued to be.

I headed for the kitchen and a further chat with Chef Victor Gontier.

CHAPTER TWENTY-SIX

He was up to his elbows in chicken chopping. He was not doing it himself, of course, but supervising a young woman who was evidently a novice.

"That's right," he was saying. "First, remove the right leg, then the right wing . . . turn it on its right side and remove the left leg. Now remove the left wing . . . that's it, now cut away the fillets on either side. Now cut the carcass in half. Good. Remember that the carcass, the neck, the head, and the feet all go into the stock."

He turned to me. "We have to train our own staff," he said, "it's so difficult to find good people."

"I hear the same complaint everywhere," I told him. "Still, you shouldn't have trouble finding young people who want to work here. It's a great opportunity for them to learn their trade under a chef of your renown."

He gave a Gallic shrug but the compliment registered.

"Madeleine was telling me you've been looking at the serving of eels," I said.

"That's right. I think we can make good use of them. The idea of cooking them in the fireplace where the guests can see them being prepared is a good one."

"That was Madeleine's suggestion," I told him. "Maybe it could be extended to other dishes. Guests would enjoy seeing haunches of meat and gamebirds roasting before the fire." It would cut down on the work in the kitchen too, I thought, but I left it to him to make that inference.

He nodded. "In the old stables buildings, we have a lot of stuff in storage. Iron pots, large and small, ladles, skimmers, tongs, forks, hooks, and andirons. They are wrought iron and very decorative; they only need cleaning up a little."

"Perfect," I said. "I had a further notion for your consideration. I know you must be familiar with a Salomongundy. I believe it was originally French."

"I know of it," he admitted cautiously. He broke off to correct the trainee, "No, no, Edna, when it cuts like that, the knife needs sharpening. Always use sharp knives."

He apologized for the interruption. "They have to be watched every minute. Yes, the Salomongundy, a sort of hors d'oeuvre with contrasting sharp and bland ingredients. I believe they used all kinds of meat, fish, and chicken, with cheese and vegetables, as the bland items, and anchovies, onions, and pickles as the sharp."

"Absolutely right. It's an excellent way to use remains from other dishes. Decorated with fresh herbs on a large platter, I'm told it can look spectacular. I don't think I have ever seen it. In fact, I'm surprised that no one has revived it," I said, "though I suppose some modern hors d'oeuvres trays owe something to it."

"We are going to make that Quaking Pudding you mentioned," he told me. "Madeleine has some ideas on it. She'll be here any minute, she can tell you what she has in mind."

"Good. There's another pudding, even older, back to Anglo-Saxon times, that you might consider. Steamed Carrot and Barley Pudding."

"I don't think I know that one."

"Barley was the main cereal crop in those days, so it appeared in a lot of dishes. It's quite simple. You just simmer barley, carrots, honey, and apple till the barley has absorbed most of the water. You purée it, adding mint and beat in an egg for each person. You put this in a pudding basin, steam till it rises and is firm. When it was served, quince jelly or redcurrant jelly would be spread on top."

The door banged as Madeleine came in, arms full of produce.

She dropped it all on a convenient countertop. "I love to use quince," she said. "What was that recipe again?"

I told her.

"That should be popular," she said. "The English taste still runs to puddings and people don't make them at home any more so they enjoy them when they go out. Tourists from other countries think of puddings as typically English, so they would want them too."

"I don't know if he mentioned it to you," I said, "but Victor and I were discussing berries earlier. We could make jellies and jams from them. And they would be good for putting on top of the puddings."

They both agreed. "Miss Felicity had us making jams for sale in the gift shop," said Madeleine, "using berries from the Plantation. But then the demand got too great and we couldn't grow enough. But making jellies from them to put on puddings would be perfect."

"By the way," I added, "the venison from the culling—presumably it's hanging?"

"But of course," Victor said.

"So it will be ready in a couple of days, won't it? We can make good use of that."

We made plans for cooking the venison, which Gontier said was always popular and considered a real medieval treat. It would be even more so if the guests could see it turning on a spit.

Victor turned to cast a critical eye on Edna's chopping technique. Her rate of chops per minute had increased noticeably. He gave her an approving nod.

"I have to go to the storeroom," he said, "some problem with the inventory. Madeleine, tell him about your ideas on the Quaking Pudding."

He left.

"Well," Madeleine said, "that pudding . . . I thought that we might increase the amount of both breadcrumbs and almonds. That would make it less wobbly. Then in keeping with the trend for healthier foods, we could cut down on the cream and replace part of it with yogurt."

"Excellent ideas," I agreed.

"Then there's the preparation. They used to steam puddings always in the old days. This one would be ideal for microwaving. Of course, we wouldn't let the guests know about that."

"Of course not. Let them think it's been steamed for four hours."

We talked on about other dishes, then I made a half turn to leave. It was a Columbo-style prelude to departure.

"You do a great job here in the kitchen," I told her. "Aside from cooking for all the guests. Those stuntmen seem to have tremendous appetites."

"They eat more than the horses, I tell them," Madeleine said with a smile.

"It's good to see how you all get along together so well," I went on. "You must get to know their likes and dislikes."

"Oh, we do. Of course, some of the serving girls—the wenches, as they call them—know them better than we do."

"I suppose the stuntmen all like hearty dishes of meat and potatoes best," I ventured.

"Most of them."

"Then there's Richard Harlington—he has his preferred dishes too, I suppose."

"He likes to eat a salad before he goes to a joust or do some kind of battle," she said, still in a chatty mood.

I tried to keep the conversation the same way. "Not the same one surely? I would have thought he's the type to like variety."

"I think it's always the same one. Louise would know more about that than I do. She's the head server." She gave a meaningful smile. "She has a crush on him."

I wondered how long Richard had been seeing Jean Arkwright. Would Louise have felt jilted or at least slighted? Not nearly enough motive for murder surely . . . but how much was there I did not know?

I nodded. It indicated that I couldn't care less about the romantic intrigue at the castle. "What do you recommend for lunch?" I asked her, making it clear that this was a much more important question.

Her recommendations were good. *Gemelli,* the twirled pasta shapes, had been cooked in a large volume of salted water. Salt enhances the flavor of the pasta and helps the water return to a rolling boil more quickly. It is easy to tell when this has been done as the pasta has no tendency to stick.

While still hot, it had then been tossed with minced garlic, parsley, basil, hot red pepper flakes, olive oil, wine vinegar, and *bocconcini,* bite-sized lumps of mozzarella cheese.

"It's almost as easy and much more satisfying," Madeleine had said, "to cook pasta the proper way." I was now learning that she certainly knew the proper way.

Tempting as many of the other dishes were, I managed to resist, and concluded the meal with a dessert of bananas and nuts.

I took a stroll through the grounds and met Neville Wood-ward, the cousin to whom Angela had introduced me. He had that same languid air that I had previously attributed to his noble background, though now I suddenly wondered about that. Was his apparent nobility only a pose?

"How's the foreign trading?" I asked affably. "Is the guilder going great or is the florin floundering?"

The sneer that I had suspected before was still lurking. Perhaps it had been a seesaw morning on the exchanges.

"Good days and other days," he said as if he did not want to talk about it.

"Tomorrow should be one of those good days," I said brightly. "The Battle of Moreston Marsh followed by a banquet. Can't ask for more than that."

He looked as if he were going to ask for a great deal more than that. Deciding I could not help him get it, he curled his lip. "They love play-acting here."

"Brings in the crowds," I reminded him.

"Bloody proletariat."

"They pay the bills. The castle couldn't stay open without the—er—the people." I was being mildly argumentative in the hope that I could learn more about him and his views.

"I'd run it without all these milling hordes," he said. Maybe he was nobility, after all. He had the attitude of a lord of the manor . . . from five hundred years ago.

"It would be a tough proposition," I said cheerfully. "It costs twenty-five thousand pounds a year just to control the woodworm."

He grunted something, but I couldn't tell whether he was sneering at a paltry twenty-five thousand or expressing distaste for woodworm.

"I don't think I'd want the job of running the castle," I told him. "Too many headaches. Still, we're all different. You'd probably enjoy it." I didn't think that for a minute, but it did pry a response out of him.

"I probably would," he said, lifting his chin. It gave him a Mussolini-like appearance that would have alarmed the serfs.

"Are you taking part in the battle?" I asked.

"I do from time to time," he said, and I waited for a yawn to accompany the comment. Instead, he said, "But I have better things to do tomorrow."

"Got to keep chasing those euros, I suppose?"

"Bank of Peru, actually."

He tossed the name out as he walked off. I tossed a "Good luck!" after him.

CHAPTER TWENTY-SEVEN

The morning of the battle dawned hazy and only just dry. As it was just a reenactment, weather conditions were important only from an entertainment and profit point of view, not a matter of life or death.

I felt I needed extra sustenance to face the looming conflict, so I had two eggs, bacon, sausage, and a slice of black pudding. Norman gave me a perfunctory wave from another table. Angela was not far away, but she had her back to me. Felicity came in, spotted me as I was about to leave, and came over to sit with me.

"Have any plans for watching the battle this afternoon?" she asked.

"My number one plan is to stay out of the way of stray arrows. I heartily recommend that you do the same."

"I'll make you a deal. We'll sit together. You extend to me the protection of your plan for avoiding arrows and I'll fill you in on the history of the battle and give you a running commentary on who's who—as well as who was who."

I accepted. We agreed on when and where to meet. Felicity left and the room emptied soon after. An hour later, I was still there.

Screens were stacked for the use of groups who wanted some privacy. I had moved one and set it by a corner table where I could see and not be seen. After a while, serving girls came out and set the tables for lunch. Time passed.

Large trolleys suddenly came rattling in and the buffet trays were quickly filled. More time passed. The place was quiet. Then a serving girl came in, blond hair tied on top of her head. She carried a Styrofoam box. She looked around carefully, then went to one of the buffet tables. She opened a door to one of the refrigerated shelves below, placed the box inside, and left.

I waited a full fifteen minutes, went over, and took out the box. It contained a salad. I sniffed it very carefully, then put it back.

I had eaten at a more leisurely pace than usual. That ensured that meals had been served and eaten and the staff was now clearing away. Looking over them was a pleasant task; all were young and lively and eager. But I wasn't auditioning for the chorus, I was looking for Louise.

The blond hair tied up on the top of her head made her easy to find. She had a fresh look and bright eyes. She gave me a questioning glance as I approached her. "I'd like to talk to you for just a couple of minutes," I told her.

"All right." She wiped her hands on a paper towel and led the way to a table that had been cleared. "Did you want something special from the kitchen?"

"No. I'm here to advise on modifying the menus, make them more medieval, increase business," I explained as I introduced myself.

"I know," she said. She smiled shyly. "We gossip a lot here—all girls together. Any new faces that are here more than a couple of days . . ."

"Good, then you know who I am. I wanted to ask you about salads."

A momentary flicker passed across her face but I could not interpret it. Its very presence told me a lot, though.

"Some of the regulars have their favorite foods, I know. Does anyone have a favorite salad?"

She hesitated. "Well, Mr. McCartney likes blue cheese on his so we put out a bowl of that. The foreman of the maintenance team likes lots of croutons so we put out extra of those."

"I didn't mean on the buffet," I said gently. "I meant individual servings."

"The kitchen does all that. I'm just serving staff," she said, perhaps a little quickly.

"Don't worry," I told her. "Anything you tell me will go no further."

"Is this something to do with Kenny?" Her face changed and her tone sharpened.

"It may be," I agreed, "but it need not involve you. Just tell me—"

"I didn't do anything wrong!" Alarm showed plainly in her eyes.

"I'm quite sure you didn't and you won't get into any kind of trouble." I kept my voice placatory. "But your answers may save Richard Harlington's life."

The alarm grew. "Is he . . . ?"

"He's fine but he may be in danger. What can you tell me that will help him?"

Madeleine's comments and the words of the stuntmen had set me on this track and I wasn't sure how to get the information out of this young woman. Telling her that his life was threatened had seemed like a good idea. Was it enough?

I decided to throw caution to the winds and make a wild stab. "Some of the girls prepare an occasional special dish for one of their boyfriends, don't they? You do, too—you prepare a salad for Richard before he jousts. What do you season it with? Coriander, dill, mustard, cloves?"

At least two and maybe three of those guesses registered. She did not yet have sufficient experience at evasion. I went on before she could speak.

"I told you there will no trouble for you of any kind. I mean that."

"Is it true Kenny was poisoned?"

"It looks that way but it's not certain yet. In any case, I know you had nothing to do with it."

She shook her head violently and her blond hair trembled. "I just made a special salad for Richard every time he was going to joust. I made it the way he likes it—with coriander, cloves, and dill. I put it in a chilled compartment under the buffet table so no one else would take it."

Three spices that were strong enough to cover the taste of the owlsfoot. It might have been wolfsbane, but owlsfoot sounded more likely. Both have a bitter taste.

"Kenny knew you prepared that salad for Richard, didn't he?" I asked.

She nodded.

I had a further thought. "Frank knew too." She didn't respond but I knew I was right. "But he didn't say anything because he didn't want to see you blamed."

"I wasn't to blame, I only—"

"I know. I know. I'll see to it."

I spent a few more minutes setting her mind at rest. When I left, she was back to her normal cheerful demeanor. My mind wasn't at rest, though. Someone else had known about the salad. They had awaited their chance and put owlsfoot in it.

My stroll outside was made more difficult by the activity. Seating was being erected, speakers installed on poles; vehicles of all kinds buzzed and roared, and people toiled everywhere. I returned for lunch, and, being among the earlier eaters, I was able to check quickly and find the Styrofoam box still in place. A few sniffs confirmed my previous finding.

After that substantial breakfast, I limited myself to a slice of quiche and an apple for lunch, and an hour later I was sitting with Felicity in the rows of seats erected especially for the event. Extra flags fluttered from the battlements of the castle behind us and huge colored streamers on the walls gave it a flamboyant air. A good crowd had gathered and the speakers were playing martial music that sounded like the work of Sir William Walton.

"You know something of the history of the castle, don't you?" Felicity asked.

"Just the brochure," I said. "Fill me in."

"All right. It starts with Ethelfleda, the warlike Queen of Mercia. She built a wooden fortress on this site in about A.D. 916 as defense against marauding tribes from South Wales. Sometime during the following century, it was expanded to a motte and bailey—"

"Translation please," I requested.

"Oh, sorry. A motte is a wooden tower perched on top of a mound of earth and surrounded by wooden palisades. A bailey is an outer court with another palisade around it. In 1068, William of Normandy, after his conquest of England, decreed the castle to Henry of Donningford. This was unusual as most such bequests were made to Norman knights." Felicity smiled. "We surmise that Henry was an English traitor."

"A blot on the escutcheon—isn't that the phrase?"

"Very appropriate. The period from 1100 to 1300 was the period of building—castles and cathedrals all across Europe, well over a thousand of them."

"Wasn't that because builders had just discovered how to use stone blocks?"

"That's right. Stone and brick. John of Lakeland came back from the Crusades and Richard the Lionheart rewarded him for his loyalty by giving him Harlington Castle. It was John of Lakeland who enlarged it enormously and gave it walls twenty feet thick. I could go on—it gets to be a catalogue of names, dates, and battles."

"At least tell me about the Battle of Moreston Marsh," I said, "so I know which side to cheer for."

She gave me a frown of mock reproval. "This is not a football game, it's a historical pageant."

More spectators had arrived by now and the seats were all filled. The sky had cleared and some fuzzy white clouds cruised gently at high altitude. The stirring music was appropriately that of a prelude to battle.

"The scene of the Battle of Moreston Marsh is as follows:

about 1460, the Manor of Harlington was granted to Robert Courtenay by Henry the Sixth," Felicity began. "Robert was a rich Bristol merchant and a direct ancestor of my father. His daughter married the grandson of a previous owner of Harlington Castle and so pushed back the connection between family and castle. Now here's where the intrigue sets in—"

"Good," I said. "I love intrigue."

"Richard of York determined to depose Henry the Sixth and proclaim himself king. The queen, Margaret, was quite a warrior herself and gathered an army to meet Richard in battle. But Richard had moved fast from the north and he headed for London. In his path lay one obstacle . . ."

"Don't tell me. Harlington Castle."

"You're good at this, aren't you?" She smiled.

"But why is it called the Battle of Moreston Marsh?"

"The land on this side of the castle was marshy in those days. Some of the attackers were caught in it. The major part of the battle, though, was right here in front of the castle."

"So now you've brought me up to date?"

"Yes. What happened next will be reenacted—here they come now, Richard of York's army," she said. The land in front of us fell away gently, rolling green grass with an occasional stand of trees. From that direction, an insistent drumming was audible. It persisted, then grew steadily louder. Splashes of color came into sight, battle flags in blue, green, and white. They became taller as if they were rising out of the ground.

A shrill blare of trumpets sounded, an explicit threat augmenting the menace of the drumbeat. A line of cavalry came trotting into sight, armor gleaming, lances high and the richly caparisoned horses snorting as if they smelled blood.

"In the original battle," Felicity said, "we think there were twenty rows of cavalry with at least forty men in each row."

Her words startled me. I had become lost in the past and the magnificent display had assumed a striking if transitory reality.

"We can't run to that many today, neither horses nor riders.

As it is, we have to coopt the local riding club, the county fox-hunters, and the Hertfordshire polo team."

The cavalry was in full view now, riding toward the castle. Behind them came several rows of infantry, some with swords, some with pikes in hand. Horsemen detached themselves from the ends of the ranks and galloped out, bright-colored scarves and sashes flapping.

"They are the officers," Felicity said.

"Where are the defenders?" I asked.

"We have to take some liberties with history," she said. "A few years back, we had some siege weapons built, but one collapsed and crushed a man's arm, so we've dispensed with that. Now we show the cavalry and infantry part of the battle."

Even as she spoke, the castle gates swung open and a troop of horsemen came racing out. Flags rippled, swords came out of scabbards, and the hoofbeats were a dull thunder on the drawbridge over the moat. It was an impressive scene.

"You should be filming this for a—" I started to say as Felicity pointed to where a battery of cameras already whirred at the foot of the castle walls.

Ahead of the defending troops, a horse and its rider pulled out and I could see a pennant fluttering wildly. It was the scarlet, black, and gold of the Harlington family.

"That's Richard," breathed Felicity.

The attackers were urging their steeds into a gallop now. The crowd was completely silent as the two armies charged at one another.

They met with a clash of steel that echoed off the castle walls like a thunderclap. Then they were fighting man-to-man, sword against sword, the horses prancing and weaving, and death a heartbeat away.

Severed limbs and gushing blood were not necessary, for the battle scene had a ferocity about it that was chilling. There was a sudden roar from the crowd. Felicity grabbed my arm. "It's Richard! My God, he's down!"

The figure in the armor with the scarlet, black, and gold insignia had taken a powerful blow from an adversary and fallen from his horse. We could no longer see him. He was hidden by a milling throng of horses and clouds of dust.

I felt a hand clasp my shoulder. I turned. Another hand was on Felicity's shoulder. We both looked up to see a mischievous grin on the face of—Richard Harlington.

He squeezed in between us. Felicity's face was still white. "Richard! You're all right!" Her expression changed. "But who's that out there?"

"That's Frank Morgan. Don't worry about him. We rehearsed this. Look, there now—see, he's on his feet."

We watched as the armored figure stood erect, swung his sword, and unhorsed one of the rebel army. Then he climbed into the empty saddle and rode into the throng.

"So . . ." said Felicity. The color was returning to her face. "You saw reason for once. You also scared us to death!"

He laughed boyishly. "Not to worry, sis. We spent days working all this out."

"So why aren't you in it?" Felicity demanded. She was becoming increasingly angry now that her concern was banished.

"Oh, I don't know," Richard said. "Comes a time when you have to give up doing it and be content with planning it."

"I doubt if it was anything I said," Felicity commented tartly.

"It was Frank who persuaded me actually," Richard said, intently studying the movements of the combatants.

The battle continued until the attacking army fled in confusion. The crowd booed them off the field. The victors celebrated with a triumphal ride past as they returned to the castle. The music rose to a crescendo as they disappeared inside the gates.

The people left the seats and moved inside the castle grounds, where minstrels, clowns, stilt walkers, jugglers, mimes, conjurers, magicians, and animal acts entertained them. A band played musical comedy hits and Daniel's cuddly Dancing Bears put on one of their most endearing performances. I was glad we were not going to eat them.

I stayed where the crowds were thickest for the rest of the afternoon. I even watched a Punch-and-Judy show. Finally, it was time to get bathed and dressed for the evening banquet. Before I did, I phoned a friend in one of the larger financial institutions in the City of London.

CHAPTER TWENTY-EIGHT

Half an hour before the banquet, I sauntered casually through the room where places had already been set. The large tables were resplendent with gleaming white tablecloths, polished crystal, and glitteringly bright silver. Candles had just been lit and their flames sent shadows flickering among the rafters in the high ceiling. The only persons present were two or three waitresses in pristine uniforms, setting out tall, wooden salt and pepper shakers.

I checked the seating nameplates. I was at the table with members of the Harlington family and several others whose names were not familiar. That was good, but I needed further advantage on my side. When the waitresses were occupied at a distant table, I made a rapid switch of two of the nameplates. I strolled next to the serving bay where the carts stood ready to receive the dishes from the kitchen. It looked very unlikely that any individual could control the distribution of the dishes to the tables. Still, I could see the bay clearly from my new place.

I went into the anteroom where cocktails were being served and most of the guests were already assembled. I accepted a Pimm's Number One from a passing waiter and talked with one of the members of the Stony Stratton Hunt Club. He had been one of the rebel cavalry and I consoled him on his defeat.

"You can't win them all," he said with a laugh.

"If you repeat this every year," I said, "you don't win any of them. Must be frustrating."

"One of these years, we'll have to rewrite history."

A good-looking woman in a striking purple gown said she was headmistress of the Stony Stratton Village School. I told her she was lucky to have a castle so handy. It must be useful in teaching history, I suggested to her.

"It tends to be taken for granted," she said, shaking her head sadly. "Adults recognize the gap of a thousand years, but children don't accept the time difference so easily."

The mayor was out of town, but his deputy chatted affably. He was a wispy man with sparse hair and lively as a cricket. He dropped his official role and became interested in my work once he had asked me who I was and what I was doing here. After I gave him the ostensible answer, he wanted to know why his homemade tomato sauce never tasted as good as the supermarket variety.

"In the past, homemade sauces tasted better," I told him, "because they allowed the sauce to cook for three or four hours. Today, we don't have time for that, so the standard way of off-setting that slightly sharp uncooked taste is to add some brown sugar."

"Doesn't that make it sweet?"

"Only if you add too much. Start with a little and keep adding if you need more. Give it a few minutes after each addition to absorb the sweetness. Another way," I added, "and one of my secrets, is to add a spoonful of orange marmalade. It contains about fifty percent sugar so the sweetening result is similar but the richness of the orange flavor adds to the richness of the sauce and the fruity touch improves it further."

He was pleased with that and was about to tap me for further insider tips, but I beat him to it. "You must be concerned about these two accidental deaths recently. Are they keeping visitors away? It's beginning to sound as if Stony Stratton is a dangerous place."

He looked concerned. "We haven't seen any influence on visitors' numbers so far, but I do hope that the people who keep telling me these things come in threes are wrong."

"A doctor dying in a neighborhood is always distressing. Patients like to think of their doctors as being next to immortal."

"Yes," he agreed. "In addition to that, Dr. Wyatt was very popular in the village."

"The villagers will miss her," I sympathized.

"Well, actually, no. Not from a professional point of view, that is."

"I don't understand," I said.

"Her offices are in Harley Street—in London. She lived here in Stony Stratton because she enjoyed the quiet village life."

"Oh, I see . . ." I didn't entirely but I was going to dig until I did, so I left my comment dangling in the air.

"After all," he began to explain, "Stony Stratton would hardly have any patients likely to need Dr. Wyatt's services, would it?"

"Why not? Was she a specialist in some medical field?"

He might have a wispy appearance but his gaze was keen. Fortunately, he enjoyed a bit of gossip too. That was probably an inseparable component of the village life. He studied me for a moment. "Yes, you could say she was a specialist." I waited, but he was not that much of a gossip.

I thought back. I had seen her twice at the castle. She had appeared to have a close relationship with Sir Gerald. I recalled my earlier thought that maybe it went as far as to have a romantic basis. His honor's deputy disappointed me at this point. "A sensitive vocation," he commented.

"Did you have anything to do with the meal this evening?" he asked, changing the subject quickly.

Changing the subject back was not feasible and, anyway, he had brought my hobbyhorse out of the stable. I had to admit it. "Our aim was to recreate, as far as possible, a meal that might have been served in the early 1400s, that is to say, the time when the Battle of Moreston Marsh was fought. Sir Gerald wanted it to be a formal dining occasion, however, and this presented something of a conflict. So we compromised. We're not having the rough wooden tables, we're not having the seating on one side of the table only—as was the custom then—and we're not eating with knives only. The meal, on the other hand, is authentic."

We were probably each competing to bring up our own topic when a gong resounded. "Ah," he said, "dinner. I'm looking forward to this."

I hoped I was being paranoid. Surely there would not be an attempt at poisoning here?

I made a pretense of looking for my nameplate. I was seated next to the young pretty wife of the captain of the polo team. He too, she informed me, had been one of the rebel cavalry.

"Lot of rebels at dinner tonight," I observed. "Sir Gerald must be relieved that they were defeated."

On my other side was a matronly and still attractive woman. She told me that she and her husband, president of a major insurance company and recently retired, had bought a manorhouse adjacent to the Harlington estate. Richard was on the opposite side of the table and a few seats down. It was the way I had arranged with my nameplate adjustment and I was able to look over his shoulder into the serving bay.

Sir Gerald was down at the head of the long table. Felicity was two seats away, wearing a silvery white creation with a flowing motif that made her look like Queen Titania prepared for nuptials in the Forest of Arden. Angela was the other side of me on the opposite side of the table. The two-tone brown outfit she was wearing was demure, but only superficially. She gave me a mischievous glance and her lips moved. As near as I could make it out, she was saying, "Ferns!" Her glance turned into a hot, lingering stare.

Her brother Norman was in conversation with the deputy mayor and Neville Woodward was absorbed with a voluptuous brunette.

The meal began with a "Caudel of Muscils." This was a dish that I had suggested to Victor and he had prepared as requiring only minor modifications from one of his native French dishes. It was a soup, using mussels, that was often found on medieval menus. The mussels are boiled, then braised onions and leeks are added. Ginger, saffron, cloves, and pepper are the spices, vinegar gives it a tang, then milk and chopped almonds are added.

I watched like a hawk. The dishes came out of the kitchen and into the serving bay on trolleys. The table waitresses took them from there and brought them to the table. There was no way Richard's—or anyone else's—dish could be isolated. As we were finishing this course with its blended fragrance of cloves and ginger, the wife of the insurance company president began telling me of her problems in adjusting to village life after many years in an apartment in Belgravia. I gave her lots of commiseration and then brought up events in Stony Stratton. I started at the point where the deputy mayor had become reticent.

"—a terrible tragedy," I concluded. "Although I suppose being a newcomer, you haven't been exposed to village debate?"

She smiled. "Gossip, you mean? Oh, but I have. The estate agency lady we dealt with is an endless source of information. I know as much as the old-timers who have been here fifty years or more."

Trout was the next course. This has been a favorite fish for centuries and methods of cooking it have not changed tremendously. Victor and I had agreed on a stuffing of herbs with a little lemon. We used parsley, thyme, rosemary, and nutmeg with the breadcrumbs and egg yolks. The stuffed fish was laid in a pan with white wine and fish stock. It was boiled, then removed. A mixture of flour and cream was stirred in to thicken the sauce, which was then poured over the fish.

Potatoes had not yet been brought to England at the time we had set the meal, so we did not include them. Bread was more commonly eaten in those days, so Victor and I had his pâtissier bake some "Wastels Yfarced." We discussed having The Muffin Man bake them for us, but decided we would bake them in the castle kitchen as the order was not large.

Wastels Yfarced were wholemeal brown loaves, served to the gentry and considered one of the highest quality breads. The original recipe called for cooking the loaves in beef broth, after they had been stuffed with mushrooms, spinach, and raisins, but we agreed this was not to current taste so the loaves were baked crispy instead.

I managed to keep the conversation going while watching the serving bay closely. Again, there was no possibility of any skulduggery. During this surveillance, I noticed that Richard seemed to be very friendly with the young woman next to him. She had light red hair and an aristocratic nose. When we were partway through the trout course, I went back to my interrupted conversation with the insurance president's wife. "I'm glad the village tragedy didn't affect the purchase of your house," I said. "I suppose your estate agency lady must have known the doctor."

"Yes, indeed. She's a source of knowledge about everyone in the district. She knew the doctor very well."

"Some kind of specialist, wasn't she?" I asked. "I thought I heard she had a practice in Harley Street."

"Dr. Wyatt was a psychiatrist."

I digested that gem of information along with my trout.

"She was a regular visitor at the castle, I believe?"

"She attended Lady Harlington for some time before the poor woman had to be committed to a mental hospital," the woman said. "Dr. Wyatt normally treated her patients at her Harley Street offices, yes, that's right. But she knew the Harlington family well, and when poor Lady Harlington began to have her mental problems, I understand that the doctor came here to treat her."

That cleared the air a little. It explained why and how a connection might have been initiated between the doctor and Sir Gerald. It also spoiled the notion of a romantic rather than a professional reason for the doctor's visits to the castle. But then the words of Francis Somerville, Knight Pursuivant, came back to me. Sir Gerald, he had told us, had only six to twelve months to live. He might have a need for some psychiatric counseling and that might be the answer to Dr. Wyatt's visits to the castle.

But it left a murky air of doubt about any link with the death of Kenny Bryce. What could Dr. Wyatt's death, if it were not an accident, possibly have to do with Kenny's death, even if Kenny had been poisoned in error for Richard Harlington? Before turning my attention back to the meal, I looked at Richard again. He was getting along famously with the red-haired girl.

Victor Gontier prided himself as a wine sommelier too and I let him select the wines for the meal. For a Frenchman, he had a surprisingly democratic attitude toward English wines. The fickle English climate is not kind to the country's determined band of wine growers, but with the soup and fish courses, Victor served wine from the David Carr Taylor vineyard in Kent. There, they had planted the best stock on the market. That was necessary as most varieties will not ripen even in the best of English summers. The Geisenheim stock from Germany had been selected and had achieved a deserved reputation. Complimentary comments were being exchanged around the table on this flavorsome, well-balanced Reichensteiner.

Angela caught my eye again and we exchanged what could have been intimate looks—as far as one can be intimate across a dinner table. I felt eyes on me from another direction and found Felicity smiling invitingly. They are trying to congratulate me on the meal, I thought. I hoped I was wrong.

Crustade of Partridge was the next course. A crustade is a pastry case filled with meats, eggs, and spices. In medieval times, cooks would have used much less partridge than we used here. We had added mushrooms to this.

Partridge can be tricky to handle—if hung, it can quickly become toxic. These birds had been promptly prepared—plucked, boned, and the gizzard removed. For the crustade, the traditional flaky pastry had been used, but replacing the lard with a mixture of butter and olive oil to reduce the fat content.

The venison from the recent culling was now ready, so we had very small venison steaks as the central meat course. The steaks were exceptionally moist and juicy due to having been "larded." This technique uses a large needle to sew strips of fatty bacon into the meat at intervals of about an inch.

I noticed that Victor had taken a shortcut here. He might have tried to find one of the old needles used for sewing sails, but instead, he wrapped the strips around the meat portions. The steaks had been marinated in white wine flavored with thyme, sage, and bayleaves, and the marinade saved for basting during roasting.

With the venison, Victor had not been able to resist serving a red wine from France. This one was a Hermitage wine from the Chaves' cellars. It is a wine bottled without filtration, a rarity these days. Dry, rich, and intense, it was still fruity and the snobby side of me hoped the assembly appreciated it.

The menu, printed especially for the occasion, said that we would be served Syllabub next. The wife of the polo team captain wanted to know what this was. "Syllabub," I explained, "was traditionally made by milking a cow directly into a bowl containing ale or cider. This was allowed to stand until curds formed on top of the whey. This caused problems as the curds needed to be eaten whereas the whey had to be drunk.

"Later cooks solved the problem by using wine in place of the ale or cider, and cream instead of milk. Later still, the proportion of cream was increased, and that is how it can be made today."

"Can I make it at home?" the insurance company president's wife wanted to know. "I've always wanted to serve it at a party."

"Easily," I told her. "Soak thin lemon rind in white wine for a few hours. Squeeze lemon juice into a bowl containing wine. Add the chopped lemon rind. Add castor sugar and slowly stir in the cream—using about two parts cream to one of wine. Whisk until you get thin peaks. It's best made a day or two ahead of eating."

As we finished the Syllabub, along came marble cake dark with treacle, Norfolk ginger biscuits, and thin slices of fig cake. "All popular ways to end a meal in the fifteenth century," I pointed out.

The polo captain's wife eyed these doubtfully. "Not too fattening, are they?"

"You don't have to worry."

She gave me a coquettish look. "Oh, I do. I have to watch my figure."

"Richard seems to watching a figure over there," I said. "Very closely, too."

"That's Theresa," she said, her tone becoming neutral. "Father's a judge—retired. Sir Gerald would like to see her and Richard become much closer. Take Richard's mind off that village girl."

"I suppose we don't get coffee?" I heard Neville Woodward asking. He looked down the table at me. I answered him.

"Yes, you do. We have stayed authentically to the period of this morning's battle as far as the food was concerned—"

"Except for the wines," he interrupted.

"I'm sorry you didn't enjoy them," I said smoothly, and a chorus of cries arose. Everyone had noticed how exceptionally good they were.

"We decided that as we couldn't serve wine from the period," I continued, "and as mead, ale, and cider are too heavy, we might as well be consistent with the other drinks. So there is coffee and tea—despite the fact that coffee didn't come to London till 1630 and tea a century later."

Neville looked as if he would have preferred not to have coffee just so he could complain about it, rather than have it and be forced to enjoy it. Felicity leaned forward and said to me, "That was a wonderful meal. You should be congratulated." Her smile was one of those to bask in.

"I'll pass your congratulations on to Victor," I told her. "He is responsible for the preparation and the cooking."

Angela was smiling at me, too. It was that tantalizing smile she could turn on, full of promise. These two girls were at full candlepower tonight. I wondered if there was some reason for it, but did not pursue the thought as the waitresses came round with trolleys of liqueurs.

CHAPTER TWENTY-NINE

After we had all left the table, conversations continued as guests were able to renew friendships with acquaintances who had sat too far away during the banquet.

Angela was talking animatedly with a stalwart-looking member of the polo team and Felicity was having a serious discourse with a man of decidedly academic appearance. Sir Gerald was surrounded by a group thanking him for the banquet; Neville had cornered one of the village debutantes; Don McCartney, whom I now saw for the first time, was having a business discussion with a prospect; and Norman was talking rugby with some Hunt Club members.

The polo captain's wife was making an early reconnoiter of my status and availability when Felicity appeared at my elbow. "That was Professor Gainsborough I was talking to," she said. "He's doing some agricultural research over at Huntingdon University. Cloning wheat, he was telling me. Be able to feed the whole world, he said. I asked him if he could clone caviar and he said he hadn't thought of that."

The captain's wife knew when she was outgunned and withdrew. Felicity gave me an admiring look. "Well, you really outdid yourself tonight," she said. "Everyone was very impressed."

"Thank you again," I said. "Compliments like that are hard to resist."

"You haven't seen our torture chamber, have you?"

I thought at first that I had misheard. I must have looked blank. She chuckled. "I can see that you haven't. Would you like to?"

"If it had been a bad meal—I mean, a really bad one—then I could understand being sent there. You said it was a good meal, though, so I don't . . ."

There was a merry twinkle in her eyes. "According to castle history, the chamber hasn't seen any torture for two hundred years, so you can relax. Would you like to see it?"

To be invited by a lovely girl to visit an underground chamber in a castle late at night was a romantic prospect, and my resistance to such an offer was negligible. Felicity led me through a part of the castle I had not seen before. Long corridors lined with presumably locked rooms went on and on. We went down a wooden staircase and into a vast empty room.

"They stored food in here when they were expecting a siege," Felicity told me. "Mostly grain, of course. Then they could make it into bread and they sometimes had to live on that and dried meat."

"What about water?"

"The west wing had a well. It's sealed up now but it was never known to run dry."

From there, we went down another staircase. It became colder and we entered a stone corridor, which had a damp, penetrating chill. The utter silence was almost palpable. At the end, a stone staircase, chopped out of solid rock, spiraled down.

Felicity started down it. She stopped and looked up at me. "Come on, it's quite safe." I followed her.

A dim light appeared as Felicity found a switch. The stone walls were confining and the iron barred gate ahead of us was a grim reminder of what had undoubtedly been an awful past.

"Don't you have tourists coming through here?" I asked. "This must be a great attraction, but you'd surely need more light than this."

"We did open it, some time back," she said, "but there was an accident and it hasn't been open to visitors since."

"What kind of accident?" I asked, but she was pulling open the gate of iron bars and the creaking must have obscured my question for she didn't answer.

Moisture trickled down the walls and the gloom was pervasive. The low ceiling added to the oppressive atmosphere. The sconces on the walls were torch holders and I would have liked to see all of them filled and lit. A scuttling rat or two was all that was needed to complete the melancholy scenario.

"What a place for a romantic assignation!" was the thought going through my mind when I thought I heard a laugh echoing. I had to hurry to catch up with Felicity as she turned a corner in the corridor. We went down a few rough-hewn steps and to another wrought-iron gate with a huge iron key in the massive lock. In the wall was a rusty iron lever.

The gate creaked loudly as we went through it into a chamber. A table with a white tablecloth over it stood in the middle of the uneven stone floor. On the table was a bottle of champagne in a silver bucket and some fluted glasses. On the floor was a case of bottles.

A figure bounced over them.

"Welcome to the torture chamber!" said Richard.

He poured champagne and handed us each a glass. Felicity smiled at me, enjoying my surprise. She sipped. Richard picked up his half-full glass.

"This isn't a torture chamber at all, really, though prisoners were kept down here for many years and that was torture enough," he explained. "We started coming down here when we were kids. There were no lights then and we had to bring torches."

He looked at Felicity. "Where's Theresa? I thought it was her when I heard your footsteps."

"I don't know," she said. "I thought she'd be here already." She gave him an appraising look. "Is it on again with her?"

"Might be," Richard said languidly. To me, he said, "Fine meal tonight. One of the best we've had for a long time."

"You have some talented people in the kitchen," I told him. "Some very supportive ones, too."

"Supportive?" questioned Felicity.

"Louise, for instance. She baffled the police for some time."

They both stared at me.

"Louise?" said Richard, perplexed. "Louise in the kitchen? What do the police know about her?"

"Nothing," I said. "That's the point. They didn't know that before each joust, she prepared a special salad for you and left it in the back of the cooler."

Felicity frowned. "Even I didn't know about that."

"Only one other person did—that was Kenny. He was jealous of Richard because he considered he had stolen away the affections of Jean Arkwright."

"Kenny!" Felicity said. "You mean he tried to kill Richard by poisoning the salad? Killed himself by accident?"

"Not exactly."

Richard started to say something, but Felicity interrupted. "Poison in the salad! What kind of poison?"

"An amino acid that is found in high proportions in owlsfoot—a herbal plant found in your Plantation."

Richard turned abruptly to Felicity. "Did you know about this?"

"I've heard of owlsfoot," she admitted. "It's an extremely dangerous plant. Dennis, the gardener, has mentioned it, but if we have had any in the Plantation, it has been destroyed."

Richard banged down his champagne glass. "Wait a minute! Are you saying that Louise had something to do with this? She wouldn't—"

"I'm sure she wouldn't," I cut in. "Someone else found out about her practice of preparing a salad for you. They let her do that and added some owlsfoot to it. It was unfortunate for Kenny that that was the day you decided to go into the village. He replaced you in the joust and ate your salad as a gesture of retaliation for taking away Jean Arkwright."

He was looking at me strangely. "Is this why you brought us down here?"

I motioned to Felicity. "Ask Felicity. It was her idea."

He turned to her. "What's going on here, sis?"

Her eyes were fixed on me. "Are you with the police?"

"Not exactly. I came here only to help improve your kitchens so they could serve more medieval food. I got involved in this poisoning business the day after I had arrived."

Richard was looking distinctly annoyed. "So you knew someone was trying to poison me?"

"I finally figured it out."

"Didn't you think they might try again?" He was really riled up now.

"Yes, I did. I took every precaution I could to make sure they didn't succeed."

Felicity cut in sharply. "They? Who do you mean by 'they'?"

Footsteps clanged on the stones. They were near and coming nearer.

"Theresa," said Richard, not sounding pleased. "Surely she doesn't have anything to—"

The iron gate groaned loudly as it opened.

Angela entered.

CHAPTER THIRTY

Her eyes looked bigger than ever and had an inner light of their own. She looked different somehow, like a beautiful feline ready to pounce. She gave me a provocative pout.

"Didn't drink all the champers, did you?" she asked lightly.

Richard poured her a third of a glass, let the bubbles subside, filled it, and handed the glass to her. She bowed her head archly, swung the glass to acknowledge each of us, and drank.

"Isn't this romantic?" Angela said.

Felicity's face was troubled. "Aren't we supposed to be three couples?" she asked.

Her question was directed to Angela, who pouted and drank more champagne. "In a way," she said coyly.

"What do you mean, 'in a way'?" Felicity asked. She looked at Richard and me. "Angela arranged this," she told us.

Angela emptied her glass and held it out to Richard. He examined the bottle on the table and pulled another from the case beside it. While he was opening it, Angela said, "Theresa won't be here."

"Why not?" Richard asked. "Didn't she want to come?" The cork popped. He poured and handed the glass to Angela.

"I didn't ask her."

Angela's reply startled Richard and Felicity sufficiently that they did not speak at once. Before they could do so, Angela said, "Neville will be here, though."

Felicity looked uneasily at me.

"This seems to be a family affair," I said pleasantly. "I think you'd prefer it if I left."

Angela and Felicity spoke together. Both said, "No." They looked at each other. Angela looked amused, as if enjoying some secret joke. Felicity had a puzzled expression.

Richard spoke up with the authoritative tone natural to a lord's son. "What is going on here? What do you mean, Angela? Why didn't you ask Theresa?"

Angela was not in the least disconcerted by Richard's manner. "Because it is a family affair." She nodded toward me. "He has chosen to involve himself in it so he should stay."

"I still don't understand what you're talking about, Angela," Richard said testily. "What do you mean, family affair?"

If I had to stay, I decided I might as well dive in at the deep end.

"She means the elimination of the Harlington family."

That was a show-stopping line if ever I used one. I got the full attention of the three of them. I went on while they were all still stunned.

"The owlsfoot in the salad was intended to kill Richard. The arrow that was fired was intended to kill Felicity. That puzzled me at first. I thought it might be aimed at me, but that was egotism. I knew nothing at that time so I could not have been any kind of a threat. It could have been an accident, but that was just too improbable. The most likely explanation was that the arrow was aimed at Felicity—just as the poison was aimed at Richard."

"You mean someone is trying to kill all of us?" Richard was scornful. "That's ridiculous! Who and why?"

"It was your father who supplied the key to the whole puzzle. It stared me in the face at the time, but I didn't make the connection until now—when we started talking about a family affair."

Richard frowned. "My father?"

"I suggested to him the idea of a competitor in another stately home wanting to put Harlington Castle out of business. I knew

it was unlikely. Your father called it 'too bizarre' and made a joking reference to an Alec Guinness film in which all eight members
of a noble family were killed off. This was a much easier task,
Richard—only you and Felicity."

"But just a minute," Felicity said. "There was the earlier attempt on Richard—cutting the saddle strap on his horse."

"That was a bungled and ineffective method," I said. "But it
cleared someone's mind and resulted in a decision to be more
resolute. Poison was a much more deadly means."

"The gunshot at you and Angela," Felicity said. "That was
aimed at her and not you . . ."

"It wasn't aimed at me either. You're right."

"This is getting preposterous! Who would want to kill all of
us?" Richard was getting angry and argumentative.

Footsteps clattered again on the stone-flagged floor. A figure
came into sight through the bars of the iron door.

It was Neville. He opened the door and came in.

"I see you started without me," he said.

No one offered him champagne but that was probably because
everyone present was having his or her own churning thoughts.
I know I was. When Felicity had brought me here to the "torture
chamber," I had some half-formed notions, but now the rest of
it was falling into place. I had only one regret . . . but it was no
time for regrets.

"We were talking about the Harlington family," I said to Neville cheerfully. "The immediate family really, although I know
you are a cousin."

"Half cousin to be precise," Neville said in his bored fashion.

"And to bring you up to date, we had established that an
attempt was made to poison Richard that killed Kenny Bryce by
mistake, and then there was the arrow that went astray—or so we
thought at first. It was intended to kill Felicity."

Neville regarded me for a few seconds, then his gaze roamed
around the others. "Is this some kind of joke? If so, it's in ap-
pallingly bad taste."

"There was also a gunshot that only just missed Angela," I went on, ignoring his question.

Neville's expression changed marginally. He no longer looked quite as bored. "You don't appear to have mentioned Norman," he said slowly.

"That's right, I didn't," I said agreeably.

"No attempts on his life either," Neville said, musing.

Angela turned on me, furious. "That's absurd—to think that Norman would do any of those things!"

"Then would you like to suggest who did?" I asked amiably. She stood fuming, her eyes wild.

"It was the other murder that gave it all away," I told them conversationally. "The murder of Dr. Wyatt."

"She's not part of the Harlington family," protested Richard.

"It was what she knew about the family that made it too dangerous for her to be allowed to live." I had their full attention now.

"Dr. Wyatt had been Lady Harlington's psychiatrist. The doctor was aware that she was schizophrenic just as her mother had been." I looked at Angela.

"I believe that Lord Harlington had Dr. Wyatt come to the castle to treat you. He knew that you were schizophrenic too and he suspected that you were involved in the murder attempts."

Angela's breasts heaved in anger. Her hands twitched and her face was hardly recognizable. Her enormous eyes moved ceaselessly.

"But why?" Felicity asked plaintively. "Did she hate us that much?"

"Angela has been jealous of you ever since your father married her mother. She is ambitious and sees herself as the lady of the manor. With her mother insane and Lord Harlington with only months to live, she saw her opportunity. Remove Richard and Felicity and her way would be clear."

Neville was still lounging against the iron-barred door. He heaved a sigh of boredom. "Fascinating. Fictional, but fascinating."

He heaved himself erect and said, "Come on, Angela. Let's proceed according to plan."

Angela's eyes still blazed and she looked about to erupt, but she turned and walked quickly to join Neville.

I had been scanning the chamber while I was talking. The four walls were stone. The gate with wrought-iron bars was the only entrance. The only other feature was an iron frame that fitted into one wall. It did not appear to have any function. As soon as I had that thought, an alarming possibility loomed. For the second time, I had that same regret—that no one knew where I was.

I walked over to the table and plucked a new bottle of champagne from it. I peeled the foil away. "A final drink before you go," I suggested. Richard and Felicity were looking at me in astonishment. "Now that we are all aware of Angela's ambitions," I continued, "we deserve to learn more about your plans too, Neville."

Angela glared at me. If I had had any doubts about her mental condition before, I had none know. Her contorted face looked like that of a different person. "What plans?" She turned sharply on Neville. "What is he talking about?"

I didn't give Neville the chance to speak. "Neville doesn't care about your ambition to be queen of the manor," I told her. "He's just using you. He intends to sell the castle to Leisure Holdings. You know who they are—they lost out on the contract to build the British Disneyland and so they are planning a rival, a medieval equivalent. They want to use Harlington Castle as the core attraction."

Neville might be a perfect example of the bored and indolent aristocrat but his brain moved fast. He realized it was no time to argue and that I was trying to drive a wedge between them. He pulled open the iron gate, grabbed Angela by the arm, and dragged her through. Richard showed that he was no slouch either and made a dash for the door to stop it closing.

He was too late. The gate slammed shut in his face with a metallic crash. "Don't let them lock it!" I shouted. Richard seized bars in both hands and pulled. Neville was struggling to turn the huge key but Richard managed to pull the door open an inch and it was enough to keep the key from slotting home in the lock.

Out of the corner of his eye, Neville saw Angela reaching for the lever in the wall outside the door. "No, no!" he shouted. "Not yet!" I knew then what the lever was. I still had the champagne bottle in my hand. I shook it violently and gave the cork a twist.

Eyes blazing, Angela ignored Neville and dragged the handle down. It moved smoothly and a grinding noise came from the inside wall of the chamber. The metal frame moved and the whole center section of the wall swung inward.

Water rushed in, a white cascade, boiling and bubbling, and the floor was knee-deep in seconds. The chamber must adjoin the moat and it was going to flood the chamber—the traditional way of disposing of unwanted prisoners.

Neville chopped down on Richard's fingers with the edge of his hand. Richard let go the bars of the gate with a cry and Neville seized the massive key and began to turn it.

I gave the champagne bottle another hasty shake and aimed it. The cork came out with a noise like a shotgun.

I have spent many years opening champagne bottles, always carefully holding them so as not to hit anyone. This was the first time I had taken deliberate aim. If I had had time, I would have argued that if I could miss people at will, then I could hit one at will.

The cork hit Neville in the face, just under one eye. He yelped and let go of the key. Richard promptly wrenched the gate ajar. I turned for Felicity, snatched at her arm.

The spray from the incoming maelstrom now obscured everything. We could not see one another and I had not gone more than two or three steps when the surging waves were already chest-deep. The noise reached a crescendo that deadened the senses.

CHAPTER THIRTY-ONE

On the west side of Harlington Castle, above the residential wing, a roof had been reinforced and rebuilt as an outdoor dining and lounging area. Large umbrellas kept the scorching English sun from burning those at the tables. At least, that was the fond hope, although the sun rarely cooperated.

Crenellated battlements permitted a view of the green countryside that rolled away to the horizon. It was a pleasant day, with only a few billowy white cumulus dotting the blue sky.

Felicity, Richard, and Norman sat there with me and we had gone through a number of "if only's" and "perhaps we should's."

Norman broke the silence that ensued. "From what you tell me, I suspect that Angela would have preferred to drown rather than face life. If so, she got her wish. I doubt if Neville felt the same way, though."

"The last I saw her," Richard said somberly, "she was trying to grab Neville. I couldn't see whether she was helping him or trying to save herself."

I thought that another possibility existed—that Neville was more concerned about saving himself, even if it was at Angela's expense. But I didn't say so. He had drowned too, so my speculations were irrelevant.

"You've known for some time, haven't you, Norman?" Felicity asked.

Norman looked up at the sky. "She started to show signs of uncontrollable behavior when she was eighteen. She concealed it very well."

"We were all aware of her swings of mood," Felicity said, "but we didn't realize how much further they had gone."

"You shielded her a lot, didn't you?" asked Richard.

Norman nodded miserably.

"But you didn't suspect her of murder?" Richard persisted.

Norman hesitated. "I—I was aware that she was capable of it. I knew she was jealous of Felicity, but I kept telling myself that she would never really kill anyone."

"One thing I don't understand," said Felicity, "is who shot at her during the culling?"

It was my turn to look up at the sky. "Someone who wanted to divert suspicion from her, I suppose," I said. Norman flashed me a glance, then looked away.

One of the staff arrived with a pot of coffee. She set out cups and poured.

"It was when you were away in America, Felicity." Norman said suddenly. "Angela went to the Plantation quite often. At first, I was surprised she was even interested, but then I realized she saw herself in your place. I watched her. She'd parade around the Plantation giving orders to Dennis as if she knew what she was talking about."

"Some comment by Dennis must have drawn her attention to the owlsfoot that had sprung up," I suggested. "She took an old book out of the library and read the description of it."

Norman nodded. "She must have read up on it, picked some, and squeezed out the juice."

I knew that the police had searched her room and found the incriminating book that had told her all about the deadly owlsfoot. Felicity shuddered. "I'm sorry, Norman, but I can't help feeling sorry too for those poor people who came to the castle while Angela was experimenting. None of them died, fortunately."

"I still find it hard to believe that you went to Dr. Wyatt's cottage thinking she had phoned you," Richard said to me. His tone was not exactly belligerent but it was critical.

"I had never heard Dr. Wyatt's voice." If I sounded irritated it was because Inspector Devlin had spent some time harping on the same point. "The voice on the phone did sound familiar but I didn't suspect at the time that it was Angela. When she said she was Dr. Wyatt, I accepted it."

Inspector Devlin had gone on from there to hint that the ploy to have me shoulder the blame for poisoning Dr. Wyatt might have worked had not Inspector Hemingway intervened. It was the nearest to a concession I had heard her make.

"It would have been a nice touch to have me accidentally drowned along with you two," I added. "Alleviate a lot of suspicion that you two alone were the targets."

"Thank you for not being obliging," Felicity said wryly. She sighed. "We knew, of course, that Angela and Neville were—well, were lovers. Between half cousins it's supposed to be acceptable, but still it's the kind of relationship that families tend to sweep under the carpet. We ignored it. Perhaps we should—Oh, I don't know." She turned away and I knew that despite everything, she had nurtured a strong affection for her stepsister.

"How are the preparations for the Empire Historical people coming along?" Richard asked me. He caught my surprised look. "I'm taking much more responsibility for the operations here from now on," he said. "My father has suffered enough, it's time for him to take it easy."

"It's all well in hand," I told him. I didn't think it appropriate to congratulate him on growing up. Neither did I intend to tell him I was glad he had given up the jousting or that I hoped he had finished fooling around with the village girls. "I'll be keeping in touch with Victor on that. As for the changes in the routine banquets, most have been made and I'll be back next week to confirm a few more. By the way, there are a couple of minor changes in administration I would like to suggest. Perhaps you can see they are put into practice?"

"Certainly," he said briskly. "What are they?" He sounded as if he really meant it.

"Victor should take more time away from the kitchen to check suppliers. A schedule should be set and adhered to. The supplies office should handle the arrangements for the visits and file Victor's reports. Check sheets should be prepared." I saw no reason to mention Seven Seas.

Richard nodded firmly. "I'll see to that. Anything else?"

"Tighter security at the gates. On vehicles."

He frowned. "Care to elaborate on that?"

"Better all round if I don't," I said pleasantly. I had already talked privately with Madeleine, Victor Gontier's efficient assistant in the kitchen, and referred obliquely to Roberto's restaurant in the village. A few inquiries had quickly revealed that "Roberto" was really Robert, Madeleine's cousin. The blue van had been taking him "surplus" foods from the castle kitchen where they were not missed, so as to help him in these early days when finances were tight. She was too valuable a member of the kitchen staff to lose and she had accepted my warning in the right spirit.

Richard was about to pull rank on me and demand more information, but Felicity caught his eye and in his new role he merely nodded. "One further suggestion," I added while he was in a compliant mood.

"The Muffin Man is an outstanding bakery. Much more could be done with it. A young woman called May has been running it since her father had a stroke. He didn't want his condition made public; he was afraid it might lose him business. She has a very good knowledge of the baking side of the operation, but she's weak on the business part—sales, marketing, and so on."

"What are you recommending?" Richard asked, and Felicity was listening curiously.

"I think you should buy it. The price can't be too high. If the Muffin Man does recover, have him run it for you. If he doesn't, his daughter can take over with a little help. The castle consumption of The Muffin Man's products alone would justify it and outside sales would quickly turn it into a real moneymaker."

"Sounds like a good idea," Richard said. "Unusual and different kinds of bread are popular."

"Have you got the people coming in to repair the flooding mechanism, Richard?" Felicity asked. "We don't want that to happen again, even by accident. Particularly if you're thinking about reopening it as a torture chamber."

"You hadn't mentioned that," I said. "It's an excellent notion." I finished my coffee. "Have to go," I said. "A final word with Inspector Devlin."

I shook hands with Richard and Norman. Felicity gave me a peck on the cheek, making it linger long enough to murmur softly, "I'll see you when you come back next week."

There were two of them in the hall. "Ah, two inspectors with one stone," I greeted them. Hemingway was his usual imperturbable, well-groomed self. Devlin had given her hair one stroke of a brush that had not even partly tamed it.

"We have most of what we need," said Inspector Devlin in her uncompromising voice. "I will probably want a further statement from you in the next days."

"I am at your disposal, Inspector," I told her in my most cooperative manner.

She nodded brusquely and turned to Hemingway. "Thank you for your support on this case, Ronald."

Ronald! Had it been this case that had brought them to first names? Or did they already know each other that well? Were there some things I didn't know? Had I been manipulated?

"You were correct, too," she added to Hemingway. "Your advice worked out well."

I looked from one to the other. Was I going to be let in on this?

Not by Hemingway—he gave me his tightest smile. Devlin, however, was not one to be constrained by tact or subtlety. She turned to me. "Inspector Hemingway suggested that I give you your head and you would blunder into the truth."

I had been manipulated. Devlin had known all the time of my contact with the Food Squad.

"Glad to be of help." I tried to sound bitter but it was a dismal failure. Hemingway just eyed me pleasantly and Devlin gave me her usual bleak gaze. "If my blundering can be of further assistance, just let me know," I added, doing the best I could to make it sound caustic. It was about as effective as pouring chocolate sauce over profiterolles.

"Meanwhile, I have to go," I said icily. "I need to talk to Victor Gontier before I leave."

Victor was staring at several large fish. Brownish scales glistened on their backs and golden scales gleamed on their flanks. The tiny mouths had four fleshy appendages around them.

"They're not large enough to be mirror carp," I said. "Too bad, they have the most delicate flavor. They're probably Kollar carp, almost as good. Where are they from, Belgium?"

"They are Kollar," said Victor. "They're from Seven Seas."

Well, well, I thought, so Dennis Violet is trying to hold his position as a supplier by coming up with something special.

"They probably are from Belgium," said Victor.

"What do you propose to do with them?" I asked. "Carp have been coming into England for five hundred years. They are a perfect medieval dish."

"Alsacienne? Stuffed and then poached in white wine?"

"À la juive?" I countered. "Sautéed with onions in oil, sprinkled heavily with flour, then cooked with white wine, garlic, and cayenne?"

He nodded. "Yes—or how about Polish style, cooked with red wine and ginger snaps, then served with a sauce of sugar, butter, and vinegar?"

"Hungarian style," I tossed out. "Seasoned with paprika,

placed on a bed of onions in a baking dish, sour cream, and lots more paprika and baked."

"*Matelot* style—"

"Grilled—"

"Roasted—"

"I'm surprised you haven't suggested Carp Chambord," I told him.